The Secrets
We
Keep

p. a. farrell

ISBN: 979-8-9932655-0-6

Cover photo: Orhan Pergel on Unsplash.com

Books by Patricia A. Farrell, Ph.D.

When You Can't Pour From an Empty Glass: CBT Skills for Exhausted Caregivers

The Little Book on Learning Big Critical Thinking Skills

The Smart Kid's Survival Guide: Making Good Choices in a Confusing World

How to Be Your Own Therapist

It's Not All in Your Head: Anxiety, Depression, Mood Swings and Multiple Sclerosis

Unfiltered: Beneath the noise of our thoughts lies the true narrative of our minds

Unfiltered Again: A behind-the-scenes look at healthcare, medicine and mental health

A Social Security Disability Psychological Claims Handbook: A simple guide to understanding your SSD claim for psychological impairments and unraveling the maze of decision-making

A Social Security Disability Psychological Claims Guidebook for Children's Benefits

P. A. FARRELL

The Disability Accessible US Parks in All 50 States: A Comprehensive Guide

Birding in the US NOW!: A birding guide for individuals with disabilities

Contents

Introduction

We all carry stories inside us—the ones whispered in kitchen corners, buried beneath floorboards, or hidden behind doors we've learned not to open. These stories shape us in ways we don't always understand, threading through our lives like invisible wire, connecting moments that seem unrelated until we step back and see the pattern.

"The Secrets We Keep" began in the spaces between what was said and what was felt in my own childhood. It started with fragments—a photograph tucked into a drawer, the sound of footsteps in an empty hallway, the way adults would suddenly stop talking when children entered the room. Each story in this collection grew from those fragments, from the understanding that every family, every neighborhood, every life contains mysteries that are both deeply personal and universally human.

These twenty-five stories explore the hidden dynamics that exist in ordinary places. They follow children navigating adult secrets, families bound together by what they don't discuss, and neighbors whose carefully constructed facades hide profound truths. You'll meet characters like Wally, who disappears into her own reinvention; the Bottle Babies, who survive on society's margins; and a young girl learning that protection sometimes comes from the most unexpected sources.

The collection is organized around the truth that no single story can capture everything. Memory is selective, colored by emotion and distance. Each narrator offers their version of events, their piece of a larger puzzle that can never be completely assembled. This fragmentation isn't a flaw—it's how we actually experience life, in glimpses and moments, in conversations overheard and details that stick with us for reasons we can't explain.

Some of these secrets are dark, reflecting the reality that childhood isn't always safe, that families can be both sanctuary and battlefield. Others reveal the quiet heroism of ordinary people—teachers who care for more than just their students, neighbors who offer protection without being asked, mothers who make impossible choices with grace. All of them acknowledge that growing up often means learning to carry knowledge that weighs more than small shoulders should bear.

But here's what I've discovered in writing these stories: secrets aren't just about shame or fear. They're also about survival, adaptation, and the fierce loyalty that develops between people who share difficult truths. They're about the way children learn to read between the lines, to find safety in unexpected places, to protect what matters most even when they don't fully understand why it needs protecting.

If you've ever wondered about the photograph in your grandmother's drawer, the neighbor who seemed to disappear for weeks at a time, or the conversations that stopped when you walked into the room, these stories are for you. They're for anyone who understands that the most important truths are often the ones we don't speak aloud, and that sometimes the greatest act of courage is simply learning to carry someone else's secret with the dignity it deserves.

Read these stories, and then look around your own world with fresh eyes. Notice the spaces between words, the careful way people arrange their faces, the small acts of kindness that happen when no one is watching. Every neighborhood has its mysteries, every family its untold stories. The question isn't whether secrets exist—it's whether we have the courage to handle them with care when they're finally revealed.

Your own stories matter. They deserve to be told, to be heard, to find their way to the readers who need them most.

Are secrets lies? If you look it up in a thesaurus, you surely won't find that they are synonyms. But when you think about it, secrets are lies that we tell ourselves and others. We withhold the information consciously, pushing it back so that we don t have to deal with some of them, and others that are too horrific and refuse to be denied their time.

Growing up in certain places, under certain circumstances, in a particular slice of our culture, we learn that lies are tools to navigate the mechanisms that drive our culture, and we use them as we tell the lies and keep the secrets to ourselves.

I often find myself wandering in that strange, dirt-floored cellar of the old farmhouse where much of my early life took place, and I look around at the walls. I am particularly drawn to and curious about the newspapers spread on one wall. They must be at least thirty or forty years old. Why would anyone put newspapers on a basement wall? There's no sign they served any special purpose. They're just there, existing just like the natural stone walls, carefully placed to form the foundation of this house that has endured. Newspapers don't hold up walls, but they do hold secrets.

I never explored the portion of the boiler room that had proven to be the bulwark to hold evil in place, even though I easily could have walked back there. But I was a child then, and children don't always exercise curiosity in a dark cellar by themselves. Sometimes that has to wait until you're much older, but then the cellar and the house are gone, and with them, all of those hidden secrets.

No, I don't live in regret for not having picked away at the newspapers or tiptoed back behind the old furnace to see what was hidden there. These were secrets for someone else, and they will be secrets forever now.

Chapter 1: The Last Feather

S he kept the photograph at the bottom of her dresser drawer, the edges curled, the ink fading. A line of young women in sequins and feathers smiled for the camera, but their smiles were as brittle as glass. If anyone asked, and some often did, she'd laugh it off, saying she never had the legs for it, that she lasted only a few weeks. That much was true. What she didn't say was why. But undefinedat least it was an escape from their family butcher shop and her father's unwelcome touches after her mother died. The family dog tried to keep him at bay, but that, too, didn't work well enough. Where was her chance to escape? It came, but not as she had hoped.

At sixteen, she thought she'd stepped into a dream. Standing beneath the hot lights of the New Amsterdam stage, she could feel the floor trembling with the applause, the chandeliers blazing overhead, and the orchestra spilling notes that made her feel like she was floating. It was magical at that moment. Costumes shimmered like sunlight on water, and the audience leaned forward as if the girls themselves were precious jewels on display. To her, a girl from Queens in New York City with no name and no money, it was a world wrapped in gold.

But backstage was another world entirely. There the air was thick with cigarette smoke curling into the rafters, powder settled on dressing tables, and the sharp, almost overpowering tang of cheap perfume clinging to the aged velvet curtains. The smiles slipped like Halloween masks as soon as the girls left the stage, replaced by quick glances and whispered warnings. No one lingered on dreams there; the stage mask was what they wore for the paying crowd. It was almost like a grim exercise they had to perform just to keep their place in line. And a place in line was all it was about. If they lost that, there would be little to hope for tomorrow.

Her roommate, Clara, was the first to hint at it. She had a way of tightening her grip on the younger girl's wrist before certain men stopped by after the show, murmuring, "Keep your head down. Don't let them notice you." At first, she thought it meant avoiding the gossip columnists or the leering stagehands. But Clara's eyes told another story, one she didn't yet understand.

It was on a Tuesday when she heard the secret she would never forget. She was in front of the mirror pinning her headdress, her sequins catching the light, when two dancers near the wardrobe racks began to murmur. Their voices were low but urgent. They weren't talking about the applause, or the parties, or the rich men who sometimes waited by the stage door. They were talking about Lillian—the girl who hadn't shown up that evening.

"She's gone," one said flatly, slipping a silk stocking up her leg. "Sent away."

"Because she refused him,'"the other added. The words were sharp but heavy and hung in the air just like the cigarette smoke, but more dangerous. Refused who? She didn't know. But the tone left no doubt: someone powerful enough to make a girl disappear with nothing more than a nod.

Her hands stilled on the pins, her breath catching. She turned back to the mirror, but the face staring back at her no longer looked like a starry-eyed girl chasing a dream. It looked like someone who had just seen the edge of the stage—and what lay beyond.

For the rest of her short run, she moved carefully. She smiled when told to, laughed when expected, and folded costumes with dutiful care. But the secret lodged in her throat like a chicken bone. Every time a patron leaned too close, every time the manager's voice hardened, she remembered Lillian's empty place at the dressing table. And she counted the days until she could leave.

One night, she didn't return. She walked out into the cold Manhattan air with her costume folded in a plain paper bag, the sequins already losing their shimmer. No one stopped her; no one called after her. She slipped into the city crowd, just another girl in a cheap, ill-fitting coat, and never went back.

Decades passed. The feathers and sequins yellowed at the bottom of her drawer, buried beneath sweaters and stockings. She married, had children, and grew old quietly in a small house with lace curtains. If anyone asked about her time on stage, she offered the safe version of a teenager's adventure, a lark that didn't last. People smiled, nodded, and moved on. The secret stayed locked within her careful words.

But on some nights, when the house was still, she pulled out the photograph. Her fingers traced the line of girls, their smiles wide, their eyes bright. And always she paused at the blank space between two figures, where she imagined Lillian should have been. She wondered what became of her, whether she'd been cast aside in some quiet scandal or swallowed whole by the city. No obituary ever appeared, and no story was told. Only silence.

Years later, her granddaughter found the photo. The girl had the same curious tilt to her chin, the same hunger for answers. "Why didn't you keep dancing?" she asked one afternoon, her eyes wide with the innocence of someone who believed all dreams were safe.

The older woman hesitated, the secret pressing against her lips as it had for sixty years. Finally, she shook her head and said, "Not everything needs telling."

Her granddaughter frowned but didn't push. The woman didn't slip the photograph back into the drawer. No, not yet. She sat in the quiet afterward, touching its edges, thinking of the feathers long gone and the ink fading, and she wondered—always wondered—what price had been paid for silence.

Chapter 2: The Giant Who Played Catch

So, there were these guys we called the Bottle Babies. Homeless men who hung around our alley sharing cheap wine bottles and sleeping wherever. Most people crossed the street when they saw them coming. Me? I knew all their faces from sitting on our back steps.

Rube was huge. I mean really huge—6'6" with farmer muscles and these massive hands. But unlike the other Bottle Babies, who were drunk half the time, Rube stayed clean. His clothes were beat up, but he washed them. Always shaved. And he actually worked real jobs that people paid him for and wanted him back.

I don't know how he ended up living in the alley. Nobody ever said and I never asked. He was just there and I liked him fine.

One day he goes, "Want to play catch?"

Picture this giant wanting to toss a baseball with some skinny kid. I ran and got my mitt— I only had one since girls couldn't be on the church team, anyway.

We're standing on these crushed cinders behind the buildings, and Rube winds up like he's in Yankee Stadium or something.

That ball came at me so fast I didn't even see it coming. SMACK! Right in the mouth.

Blood started running over my teeth and I'm tasting this weird sweet metal taste. But you know what really got me? Rube started bawling. This enormous tough guy was crying like a baby.

"Oh, Little Miss, I didn't mean it; I didn't mean it!" He's bent over me, patting my head with hands big as dinner plates, tears all over his face like he just killed somebody's dog.

I wiped the blood on my sleeve. "It's okay. Let's keep playing."

He stares at me as if I grew another head. "You want to keep going?"

"Yeah, but stand closer so you have to throw underhand."

That's how we worked it out. He felt terrible, I didn't want him feeling bad, and we both knew stuff happens.

Week later I ask him to play again and his face goes all weird.

"Can't do it this time, Little Miss. Got extra work at the fish store." He's looking at his boots now. "Don't have money this week and they said they'd pay me extra. Got to give my wife something for my boy—he needs shoes."

Wait, what? Wife? Kid? All this time I thought Rube was just another Bottle Baby with nobody. Turns out he's got a whole family somewhere. I remembered seeing him with this rough-looking woman and a little boy once. The woman had that hollow look people get when they're fighting the bottle too. But that little boy—maybe eight—wrapped around Rube's legs and got swooped up in the air, both laughing.

"How about Saturday at lunch?" Rube asks, looking guilty.

"Sure." At least he was working, not begging like the others.

Saturday comes and here's Rube out the back door of the fish store, still wearing his stinky rubber apron but grinning ear to ear.

"See? Told you I'd be here."

I spent the whole week working oil into my glove to make a good pocket. Fifteen minutes was all we had, but that was plenty. He threw underhand now like I showed him.

"Hey Rube, what if you saw somebody doing something really bad?"

"Like what?"

"I saw the painter smack a baby. Called me names too."

Rube's face went blank. His hands turned into fists and he started forward like he was going to march over there and teach that guy some manners. Then he stopped dead.

"You got to tell your mother about that, Little Miss. I can't do nothing 'cause I already had trouble with cops. I do what I want to that guy and I'll just get in worse trouble."

Made sense. Guys like Rube living on the street don't get breaks. One scrap and he loses his job, maybe goes to jail. Then what happens to buying shoes for his kid?

"Tell your mother, okay?" He's already heading back inside.

I'm walking home, crunching through cinders, thinking how this giant could probably flatten anybody, but he won't. Too much to lose.

That's when I figured out being tough isn't about how hard you punch. Sometimes it's knowing when not to.

Chapter 3: The Injury

The solid rubber ball returned with the force of a missile, striking me in the groin near the femoral artery. If you want to kill somebody, that's the way to do it. The searing pain precipitated a yell I didn't know was possible.

I shouldn't have been throwing anything in the living room—a room we never used, where no one ever sat, where furniture lived like museum pieces gathering dust. But I was bored and alone with nothing but that ball, the size between a softball and baseball, solid rubber with the weight of guilt.

My mother came running, half-angry that I'd been doing something so reckless. "What were you thinking?" But when she saw the area swelling on my inner thigh, her anger shifted to alarm.

By the time my father came home for lunch, a yellowish-filled bag the size of a silver dollar was rising from my leg. I could barely walk.

"We have to take her to the hospital," he said, trying to hide his alarm.

The emergency room doctor looked dismissively at my leg, yawning as he delivered his verdict: "Put hot compresses on it. Hot as she can stand. It will heal itself."

My parents followed his orders because that's what you do when doctors speak. They trusted the man in the white coat, even though something in my father's face suggested he didn't like what he was seeing.

The hot compresses made everything worse. The angry swelling filled with something that looked like pus, small holes opening in the top. My parents brought me back to the ER immediately.

That's when the real interrogation began.

The social worker appeared with her clipboard and suspicious eyes, leaning over my gurney like a detective questioning a criminal.

"How did this happen to you?" she asked, her voice dripping with accusation.

"I hit my leg while playing with a ball in the living room."

"What did your parents do to you? Did they hurt you?"

The question hit me harder than the rubber ball. "No, my parents did what the doctor told them to do."

"You don't have to be afraid. Tell me what they did, and they won't do it again."

But I wasn't afraid of my parents—I was afraid of her. This stranger wanted me to betray the two people who had rushed me to the hospital twice in one day, who had sat in that Plymouth outside the emergency room worrying about a leg that might need amputation.

"They didn't do anything to me," I insisted, my voice rising even as tears rolled down my cheeks. "My mother did what the doctor told her to do. I heard him tell her."

The woman's face screwed up in disbelief. "No physician at this hospital would have advised parents to apply hot compresses to this type of injury."

But he had. I was seven years old, and I knew what I'd heard. Why was everyone looking for someone to blame when the real culprit was incompetence disguised as expertise?

The secret I was keeping wasn't about abuse or neglect. It was about the fierce loyalty that small things develop when the world tries to tear apart the only safety they know. My parents weren't perfect, but they were mine. They had carried me to that car, driven through the streets to reach help, and waited in hard chairs while strangers poked at their child.

When the social worker realized I wouldn't break, she wheeled around and left in exasperation. Then came the doctors with their whispered consultations and grave pronouncements: emergency surgery, possible amputation at the hip, a lifetime as a cripple.

"Promise me you'll wake me up," I said to the nurse as they wheeled me into the elevator toward the operating room. Even at seven, I knew that sometimes people went to sleep during surgery and didn't come back.

I woke up in a ward that stretched like a football field, filled with forty sick children separated by glass partitions. My leg was fitted with a rubber drain and something called a "spike bandage"—no stitches, just an open wound that had to heal from the inside out.

For two weeks, I waited by the window during visiting hours, watching buses disgorge streams of people that never included my parents. I didn't know that my father was climbing dark stairwells after work, trying to bribe nurses with Loft's candy and whiskey just to see me for five minutes.

"I'm sorry, but visiting hours are over," they'd tell him, turning away a grieving father in work clothes who looked nothing like the well-dressed visitors they were used to.

"It was the first time I ever saw your father cry," my sister would tell me years later.

The nurses on the children's ward were angels disguised as women in white caps. They cheered our wheelchair races down polished corridors, stocked extra desserts for our midnight raids on the snack room, and never scolded us for the joy we stole from institutional life.

The meal lady was the best of all—a heavy-set African-American woman who called us "baby" and made every dinner tray feel like love delivered on a cart.

"Baby, why you not eaten?" she asked when sadness stole my appetite. "You mamma probably busy workin' or she got things at home. She know you in a good hospital and we takin' good care of you."

She sat on the edge of my bed, this woman who understood that sometimes mothers can't come even when their hearts are breaking. "Right now, you gots to be brave and help you mamma that way."

When I finally went home, my sister had saved twenty silver pennies—collected by scouring neighborhoods for deposit bottles while I was gone. She bought a clown bank that stuck out its tongue to swallow coins, and we laughed until we cried at the magic of it.

But happiness was fragile in our house. Within a month, my mother threw a carving knife at my sister during dinner, opening a gash over her eyebrow that would scar her for life. The loving woman who had rushed me to the hospital twice in one day, could also turn dangerous without warning.

I learned to be silent at dinner tables. I also learned that hot compresses could make things worse. I learned social workers saw abuse where there was only desperation, and that sometimes the people trying to help you were more dangerous than the people trying to save you.

But the most important secret I learned was about the defense of small things. Like the tiny blue crabs I'd watched on fishing piers, hanging onto seaweed-covered pilings with one claw while menacing threats with the other. Very small, yet they knew how to survive.

They taught me that small creatures can push back against massive enemies, whether real or imagined. That survival lives in your DNA and doesn't need to be taught. That sometimes the fiercest battles are fought not with weapons but with refusal—refusing to betray, refusing to break, refusing to let strangers tear apart the imperfect love that's the only love you know.

The rubber ball disappeared after I came home from the hospital. Maybe my mother threw it away, or maybe it just rolled under some furniture where solid rubber balls go to hide from the children who learn too young that play can turn dangerous, that help can hurt, and that love and fear often wear the same face.

But I kept the secret of that ball and all the other secrets that came after. Because sometimes keeping secrets isn't about hiding shame—it's about protecting the small, fierce loyalties that make survival possible, even when the world insists there's nothing worth defending.

Chapter 4: The Protectors

The pink handball made that satisfying thwack against the brick wall. One bounce, one catch. Another thwack. The schoolyard was empty except for me and the echo of rubber on brick.

"Hey, kid."

Four girls walked toward me, hands shoved deep in their windbreaker pockets. Public school girls. The kind who didn't wear frilly dresses or curl their hair with hot irons every Sunday morning. The kind whose mothers let them wear jeans to church.

I stopped throwing the ball. It felt suddenly heavy in my small hands.

"We're starting a girls' knife club," the biggest one said. Her voice carried the weight of someone used to being heard. "Want to join?"

Knife club. The words bounced around my head like my Spalding had bounced off the wall. In our neighborhood, you learned early what fear felt like in your belly. This was it—that cold twist that made you want to run but kept your feet planted to the macadam.

"Nah," I said, trying to keep my voice steady. "I just like hanging around here. Playing handball."

The leader studied me with eyes that had seen things mine hadn't. Not mean eyes, exactly. But measuring ones.

"All right. But if you change your mind, let us know."

I nodded, gripping the ball tighter.

"And kid?" She stepped closer. "If anybody gives you trouble in this yard, you tell us. We'll be around."

Protection. From girls who carried knives in their pockets like other kids carried lunch money. I should have been more scared, but something else crept in. Relief, maybe. Or the strange comfort of knowing someone noticed I existed.

"Thanks," I managed. "I appreciate that."

They drifted away as easily as they'd appeared, their footsteps fading across the macadam. I went back to throwing my ball, but the rhythm was different now. Thwack, bounce, catch. Each sound reminded me that I'd passed some kind of test without knowing I was taking it. There were others who should have been protectors but proved to be otherwise.

The memory of Coach Tim's hand slithering across my chest flashed through my mind. How his fingers had moved like something alive and unwanted. How the other coach had called him away before anyone else noticed. How I'd run home crying and told my mother I'd been thrown out of the game.

The lie had been easier than the truth. Who would believe that Tim—beloved Tim, who bought equipment for poor kids, Tim, who got his picture in the paper—would do such a thing? Coach Tim, who smelled like beer, somehow gained the adults' trust rather than losing it.

I threw the ball harder against the wall. Thwack.

Where were the protectors then? Where were they when old men called to children from behind chain-link fences, their voices honey-sweet and their smiles too wide? Where were they when coaches put their hands where hands shouldn't go?

The knife club girls understood something I was just learning. The world divided people into two groups: those who protected and those who needed protecting. And sometimes, if you wanted to stop being in the second group, you had to do things that scared you.

I thought about Ginger, who'd escaped the cold-water flats by using what she had, her body. About the boy down the block who pulled that horse wagon by himself, working from dawn to dusk because his family needed him to do it and earn money for them. About my sister's kidney-shaped dressing table where I tried on faces like masks, hoping one of them would fit.

We all found our ways to survive. The knife club girls had found theirs.

The ball bounced off the wall one more time. I caught it and tucked it under my arm. The schoolyard felt different now—not empty, but watched over. Protected.

I walked home through streets where outhouses still dotted back-yards, where kids like me picked through ash heaps for pieces of coal still worth burning. Past houses where mothers hung laundry on lines strung between windows, and fathers worked parking lots because that's what men in our neighborhood did.

At dinner that night, nobody asked about my day. That was usual because there was a rule in our house that you were to eat and not talk. Talking could be very dangerous as I had once learned while sitting at the dining room table. The incident was memorable, bloody, and kept as yet another family secret. My mother ladled thin soup into unmatched bowls while my father needled my brother with sharp words. My sisters sat silently by.

I ate quietly, thinking about protection. About the different kinds of strength people carried. Some carried it in their fists, some in their silence, some in their willingness to lie when the truth was too dangerous to tell.

The knife club girls carried theirs in their pockets.

That night, lying in the bed I shared with my sister, I stared at the ceiling and listened to the railroad train rumble past. The sound was comforting now, familiar. Like a lullaby for kids who grew up knowing the world could hurt them. But also knowing that sometimes, if you were lucky, protectors found you in schoolyards. Sometimes they offered you membership in clubs you were smart enough not to join. Sometimes they promised to watch over spaces where you played alone.

Sometimes protection came from the most unexpected places. From girls who walked with their hands in their pockets and their eyes on everything. From girls who understood that survival meant making choices that polite society wouldn't approve of.

I closed my eyes and made my own promise. Someday, when I was bigger, when I was stronger, when I knew how to carry my own protection—I'd be the one watching over empty schoolyards. I'd be the one offering sanctuary to kids who played handball alone.

The train rumbled past again, carrying its cargo of secrets through the night.

Chapter 5: The Bottle Babies

I suppose every neighborhood has its "Bottle Babies," who are called by something else but live the same kinds of lives—detached, disrespected, and dismissed. Our group was striking in that of the five, all of them had been in the military and were veterans of the Second World War. Each had his own story, and I'll begin here with a portion of one of them who was the most cantankerous, the most outspoken, and the most manipulative: The Butcher.

The Butcher hopped over to our green gate on his one good leg, his artificial pants leg rolled up and pinned with a safety pin that caught the afternoon light. In his outstretched dirty hand, he held a plain paper bag like a peace offering.

"I got this for you," he said to my mother, though we all knew he was lying. The Butcher never gave gifts. Under that filthy fedora, he always had some kind of scheme running through his head.

My mother's piercing look should have sent him away, but he draped himself over the gate, anyway. Her rule was clear: none of the Bottle Babies were permitted in our yard, and he knew it. Still, she took the bag just to get rid of him without further interaction.

"What is it?" I asked, peering into the bag at what looked like green flowers with thick stalks.

"I don't know, but I think it's broccoli," she said, holding the bag at arm's length.

I wasn't sure I wanted to try anything The Butcher had touched. Who knew how many microbes lived in those green folds? But my mother had been to the cooking classes at social services, where poor women learned to stretch their food budgets with newer, inexpensive foods they'd never eaten before.

The Butcher had gotten the broccoli as payment for helping clean the vegetable store's storeroom—a task he'd never completed properly because he was a compendium of excuses. The frustrated store owners had given up, handed him a dollar and some vegetables, and felt thankful when he left, even as he cursed them all the while.

He couldn't bring the broccoli to Mossy's Mulligan stew. That would have meant war.

Mossy ruled the Bottle Babies from his lair in the step-down doorway of a boarded-up store. A large, disheveled man with weeping sores covering his legs, he perpetually wore a torn fedora and kept his pant legs rolled up to his knees. The smell of rotting flesh hung around him like a cloud, strong enough to send working girls running when they rounded the corner looking for quick dates with the Chinese kitchen workers.

"Oh, Oh, Oh, Owwww," they'd squeal. "What the hell is that stink? Somebody dead back here?"

Spiked heels would fly as they wheeled around on the gravel, clip-clopping away between the stores. Mossy found this amusing, sending him into belly laughs that mixed with throaty coughs. But he was also disappointed—the Sneaky Pete didn't completely kill his interest in female companionship, even if he had to pay for it.

Sneaky Pete was Mossy's specialty, a brew he cooked in large fruit juice cans over a small flame. The alcoholic concoction had to be somewhere around 100-150 proof and could be lethal. Steam rose from the cans as he stirred, and he'd growl and push away the other men who came around for a taste.

"Not ready," he'd slur, issuing his decree like a king guarding his treasure.

Only a dime would get you a small tin can of it—enough to provide a coma-like existence for the next six hours. Relief in a tin can. Rest in an unoccupied doorway.

That night, we were initiated into the world of broccoli eaters. It was green, limp, overcooked, and not particularly interesting. I doubted Mossy would have accepted anything like that. The sight of broccoli would have brought on paroxysms of anger from him.

"What the hell is this you're trying push here?" The entire sentence would have come belching out in a slush of tobacco juice and poorly controlled, rotting teeth. A declaration of war thrown on the ground, and anyone with self-preservation would move back swiftly onto the gravel.

But I was exempt from Mossy's rages. He always quieted down when I was around, though I avoided him like the plague he smelled like. The other men would caution him about my presence.

"Hey, stop it. Can't you see there's a young girl here?"

He'd respond reluctantly, making growling noises but never threatening me. Still, I kept a distance between us. If I saw him in the alley, I'd give him a wide berth or turn around entirely. Except when I was the designated Chinese food buyer.

"Chicken chow mein," my parents would announce as a special treat, handing me the small kettle and one dollar. The dish was pathetic—like glop with bits of rubber bands thrown in—and it meant

I had to work my way cautiously up the alley and tiptoe past Mossy's garbage heap.

I'd run up the huge metal fire escape to the second-floor kitchen door, standing on the ledge while visions of white slavery ran through my head. I'd heard my mother talk about opium dens and how women were doped and sold. The entire kitchen staff would stop to gaze at this little white girl with the container, then they'd go back to chopping vegetables.

"What you want?" the supervisor barked.

"Chicken chow mein," I'd say in a tentative voice, handing over the dollar. Within minutes, he'd return with the filled container, a paper bag with a container of white rice, fortune cookies, and an almond cookie just for me.

"For you," he'd say as he smiled and offered the cookie to me with the bag of food.

Then came the terrifying part.

The black staircase glistened before me, two stories up from the ground felt like I was on the side of an ocean cliff. Darkness shrouded the entire flight, and I had to steel my courage not just for the height but for the dark. The dark was probably more of a deterrent than the distance. I could barely see my feet as I urged one foot before the other down the dark staircase.

"Oh, please feet, don't trip," I'd whisper to myself, starting a conversation of one to ramp up my courage. "Now it's ok, he's sleeping down there and you can get around him quietly and quickly and he'll never know."

Down the darkened staircase I'd make my way, past that awful smell again. His stronghold was just to the side of the bottom of the stairs, and I'd have to pass very close to where he surely must be. The cardboard would move, and my heart would stop.

"Please, God, if you help me, I promise to be good," I'd whisper, watching the cardboard for signs of life.

But I'd manage it. Mossy wouldn't emerge from his den, and I'd run down the dark alley with cinders flying behind me, afraid of everything that looked like spooks or ghosts or people hiding. The irregular cinders would catch my shoes, my ankles would bend, and I'd struggle not to fall—another scar was the last thing I needed. It seemed I was collecting scars from every summer vacation out on the island.

Several large clinkers would catch the edges of my shoe, sending me reeling to the left. Struggling to hold my precious cargo upright, I'd pull my leg to the side and manage to steady myself almost in mid-air, landing hard but continuing what seemed like a mile run but was merely half a block.

Once inside our house, I'd throw the lock as fast as possible.

Mission accomplished. Food delivered. Another safe trip past the Bottle Babies and their kingdom of desperation.

The secret wasn't in the broccoli or the Chinese food or even Mossy's terrible brew. It was in understanding that some people live in a world where dignity has been traded for survival, where a dime can buy six hours of peace, where a little girl has to navigate between compassion and self-preservation. The Bottle Babies taught me that sometimes the most broken people still follow their own strange codes—protecting children, sharing what little they have, finding ways to keep going when everything reasonable says they should stop.

As an adult, I'd learn about Korsakoff's psychosis and understand what Sneaky Pete had been doing to Mossy's brain, picking out any vestige of sanity and replacing it with a black void. But then, I only knew to keep my distance while still seeing them as human beings who deserved something better than Potter's Field on Hart Island.

That was the real gift The Butcher gave us with that bag of broccoli—not just a new vegetable to try, but a lesson in how kindness and fear can coexist and how we can acknowledge someone's humanity while protecting ourselves from their damage.

Chapter 6: My Block

The brass nameplate on the library door caught the afternoon light as I clutched Sweetie Pie tighter against my chest. Her pale orange rompers were freshly pressed, her real curly hair brushed until it shone. The heart-shaped tag around her neck read, "My name is Sweetie Pie" in Aunt Mary's careful script.

"Are you sure you want to bring her?" Mama had asked that morning, smoothing down my dress collar. "The other children might—"

"She wants to hear the story too," I'd insisted, and Mama's eyes had that look again—the one that said she knew something I didn't.

Now, standing before the children's section, I could hear laughter spilling from behind the wooden sliding panels. The librarian, Miss Henderson, appeared with her ready smile and wire-rimmed glasses.

"There you are, dear. Ready for story time?"

I nodded, following her through the small door cut into the massive panels. It opened like a secret passage into another world—one filled with sturdy wooden chairs arranged in a perfect circle. Children were already seated, their hands folded, their clothes crisp and proper.

"Everyone, we have a new friend joining us today," Miss Henderson announced. "Why don't you sit right here, sweetheart?"

The chair looked like something from the three bears' house, solid and welcoming. I settled into it, Sweetie Pie balanced on my lap, her button eyes surveying the room.

"Oh, I see you brought your doll," Miss Henderson said, her voice gentle but somehow too loud. "What's her name?"

The words hung in the air like dust motes in a sunbeam. Around the circle, faces turned toward me—some curious, others already smirking. I felt my cheeks warm.

"Sweetie Pie," I whispered.

The silence lasted exactly three heartbeats. Then it shattered.

"Sweetie Pie?" A boy with slicked-back hair snorted. "That's the dumbest name ever!"

"Sounds like something a baby would name a doll," added a girl in a sailor dress, her voice dripping with superiority.

The laughter erupted like a dam bursting. It rolled over me in waves, each one bigger than the last. Fingers pointed. Heads shook. Even some of the quieter children giggled behind their hands.

"That was her name when I got her," I heard myself saying, the words tumbling out desperately and shaky. "My Aunt Mary gave her to me and she had this little heart-shaped tag that said, 'My name is Sweetie Pie.' She has her own carrying case and everything. And look—real hair!"

But my voice was drowning in their amusement. I held up Sweetie Pie's arm, showing off her moveable joints, but the laughter only grew louder.

"Children, children," Miss Henderson called, but her voice seemed far away, ineffective against the storm of ridicule.

I stared down at Sweetie Pie's face—those painted blue eyes that had watched me through so many nights when the house got quiet and strange. She'd listened to every secret I'd whispered into her real hair. About how Mama's voice sounded different after Daddy came home late. About the bruises that appeared and disappeared like magic tricks. About how sometimes I pretended I was someone else entirely, someone whose doll had a proper name like Elizabeth or Catherine.

"She's the first doll I ever got," I said, but the words were lost now in the chaos.

The boy with the slicked hair was practically falling off his chair. "Sweetie Pie! Wait till I tell my mother. She'll die laughing!"

Fire crept up my neck and across my face. My fingers tightened around Sweetie Pie's soft body, and for a wild moment I wanted to hurl her across the room, to watch her smack into their smug faces and run before they could see the tears that were building behind my eyes like a thunderstorm.

Instead, I sat frozen, holding my secret-keeper while they tore apart the only gift that had ever been just mine.

"Now children, that's quite enough," Miss Henderson finally said with some authority, but the damage hung in the air like smoke.

The story that followed—something about a brave princess—blurred past me. I didn't hear a word. I just sat holding Sweetie Pie, feeling the weight of every laugh, every pointed finger, every moment when I'd thought maybe, just maybe, I could belong somewhere.

When story time ended, I was the first one out the door.

That night, I sat on Mama's bed in Brooklyn, carefully applying cold cream to Sweetie Pie's porcelain cheeks and painting her tiny nails bright red. In the mirror, she looked like a miniature movie star.

"You're beautiful," I whispered to her. "Don't listen to what they said. You're perfect just the way you are."

Sweetie Pie stared back at me with those knowing blue eyes, keeping my secrets safe as always. She understood what the children at the library never could—that sometimes the most precious things come with the simplest names, and the deepest truths are whispered only to those who know how to listen.

Outside, the world of Big Al's tavern and the shoemaker's shop hummed with its own secrets, but here in this room, with cold cream on our faces and red nail polish drying, we were untouchable.

Chapter 7:
The Unlicensed
Doctor

The pharmacy stood like a beacon on the corner of abandoned dreams, the only source of light on a street lined with boarded-up storefronts and broken promises. Mr. Himmelfarb's green-shaded lamps glowed through the night, protecting more than just his store—they protected the secret that kindness could survive in the most unlikely places.

"Hello, what can I do for you today?" His ever-present smile welcomed me as I limped through the door, another cut on my knee requiring attention.

I'd crossed from our mixed neighborhood down the hill to the African-American area, past the hand laundry where women worked half-naked in basement steam, stirring massive vats with wooden paddles like boat oars. The air down there was thick with soap and disinfectant, heavy with the sweat of women who had no choice but to endure the taskmaster who watched them like an enemy. Seated on a platform with a view of all the vats and the women working at them, the supervisor casually inspected his nails, pulled on his fat cigar and slid his roving eye over all of them; who would be next?

But Mr. Himmelfarb's pharmacy was different—a temple of mid-century healing with black, stone counters, glass cabinets reaching to the ceiling, and bottles bearing names both familiar and foreign. The elderly Jewish man in his white jacket moved through his domain with the quiet authority of someone who understood that healing wasn't just about medicine.

"Let me see what I can do," he said, pointing to the well-worn bentwood chair where I always sat. His pressed pants never wrinkled as he knelt to examine my scrape.

"Will it hurt? I don't want iodine."

"No, don't worry. We'll just brush it off with a little peroxide and petroleum jelly. Have I ever hurt you in the past?"

The secret was that he never charged us anything, either. Not once did I remember paying for his care; never was I asked for payment. He believed he was there to help people who needed help and couldn't pay for it, keeping his store in an area where both were abundant.

Enter his shop and you'd find that the real secret lived in the hair products lining his shelves—boxes and bottles featuring African-American women, advertising hair straightening and skin lightening, removing scars and changing what nature had given to them. These products were foreign to me, mysterious in their purpose, brands I didn't recognize from the pharmacies on the Avenue where glamorous white women with gleaming teeth promised beauty from ointments and cremes.

"There, you're as good as new," he said, applying the bandage with gentle precision. "Here, this is for being such a good patient." The lollipop was always part of the ritual.

"Thanks, Doctor Himmelfarb."

As I turned to leave, pulling my friend Cosmo away from whatever bottles had captured his attention, I noticed something new—a sign in the empty storefront next door: "Services at 4 o'clock this afternoon."

"Hey, not so fast," Cosmo yelled as I yanked his sweater. His voice brought Mr. Himmelfarb's head up from his compounding counter, the pestle in his hand striking the agate mortar with a soft clink before silence returned.

We crouched by the door of the abandoned store, peering through a crack in the shade. Inside, fifteen to twenty people of color, mostly women, were singing and clapping, jumping up and down, and shouting "Amen!" and "Hallelujah!" Their bodies swayed to a trumpet and drum, some women looking ready to faint from the spirit moving through them.

"Oh, those are the holy rollers, aren't they?" I whispered to Cosmo, who stared back with his typical blank expression.

We watched the celebration of faith that looked nothing like our deadly serious Catholic masses, where we contemplated metaphorical cannibalism instead of celebrating with music and movement. These people had found joy in an abandoned storefront, just as Mr. Himmelfarb had found purpose in serving the forgotten.

The secret wasn't just about free medical care or religious services in empty buildings. It was about the invisible compact that protected this corner—how the beefy men with unlit cigars emerged each night to play cards under Mr. Himmelfarb's lights, their presence guarding both the store and the neighborhood until dawn.

These men understood what the rest of the world had forgotten: that some places become sacred not because of what they cost, but because of what they give away freely. The pharmacy light didn't just illuminate a street corner—it illuminated the truth that healing happens in the spaces between official medicine and desperate need.

Mr. Himmelfarb knew what those hair products really represented—the pain of wanting to be different, acceptable, and safe in a world that measured worth by the wrong standards. But he also knew that his real medicine wasn't in those bottles. It was in the way he knelt beside a chair to tend a child's scraped knee, asking nothing in return.

The holy rollers next door knew the same secret—that salvation doesn't require fancy buildings or formal credentials. Occasionally, it just requires showing up in an abandoned storefront with a trumpet and drum, making a joyful noise in a neighborhood the world wanted to forget.

Years later, I'd learn that Mr. Himmelfarb's wife, Rosie, would die of a broken heart in a nursing home after someone stole her Tiffany Valentine's present—the gold filigree heart he'd bought her from the most expensive store he could imagine. But that tragedy had an unimaginable future.

That day, standing outside his pharmacy, I understood something simpler but just as profound: that the brightest lights often shine in the darkest places, tended by people who understand that the most important medicine is the kind you give away for free. I'd been the recipient of many Band-Aids, daubs of peroxide, and a little bit of Vaseline, plus that required lollipop, and all of it came with a soft smile, a twinkling eye, and a gentle touch.

Some secrets aren't kept hidden—they're kept alive through the daily practice of small kindnesses, through corners of the world where healing happens without payment, where joy erupts in empty buildings, where light burns through the night to protect something more valuable than merchandise.

The secret was that we weren't supposed to belong there, in that neighborhood with its mysteries and different brands of hope. But Mr. Himmelfarb and his green-shaded lights had created a sanctuary where belonging wasn't about color or class—it was about the universal need for someone to clean your wounds and send you home with a lollipop, asking nothing but that you heal. He's gone now, and so is his store. But I wonder if his spirit in the neighborhood lives on. I'm sure those men who sat all night under the streetlight with their card game think fondly of him, and I wonder what stories they tell.

Chapter 8: Wally's Mystery

Wally arrived with head cheese again, speaking German to my mother in words neither of them fully understood anymore. The jellied meat with bits of pork suspended like insects in amber made my stomach turn, but my mother accepted it graciously and threw it away the moment Wally left.

That was the secret about Wally—everything she presented was performance. The patched clothing, the thick glasses, the stumbling German she'd mostly forgotten. Even the head cheese, which she probably bought from some specialty shop, pretending it was home-made tradition when it was really just another prop in her elaborate disguise.

I watched her through the kitchen window as she struggled with her 1931 Chevy, the rumble seat car my father kept running with bailing wire and prayer. She could have bought any car she wanted—the woman had Bell Telephone stock from when it cost ten cents a share and land the airport was desperate to buy. But Wally had learned the art of looking helpless, and helpless people got things fixed for free. She'd been taught that skill of helplessness by her mentor, Nita.

"What you want, honey, it'll loosen you up," Nita had said at those Manhattan parties, pressing the glass into young Wilhelmina's hand. The butcher's daughter from Berlin had been so eager to become a lady, to escape the smell of sausage and her father's wandering hands behind the counter, she was easy pickings for Nita.

The Ziegfeld Follies hadn't lasted long. Neither had the marriage to the Wall Street banker's son who taught her about stock tips and land deals before he taught her about disappointment. But Nita's parties—those had been an education money couldn't buy.

"Look, kid, it was great," Nita had said when she left for the West Coast. "You got a great guy with banking connections. What do you want?"

What Wally wanted was someone who wouldn't leave, someone who wouldn't use her and disappear. She found that in my father, though she called him Whitey and paid him in whiskey for keeping her car running and her boat docked.

Now Whitey was gone, and Wally sat in her shack by the bay, wrapped in a shawl that snagged on the amethyst bracelet she still wore—the only remaining piece of her party days. The Persian rug from Nita's duplex lay beneath her feet, purchased for a quarter of its worth when the dream finally collapsed.

The secret was that Wally had learned to disappear long before she moved to that boarding house room. She'd disappeared the night she realized Nita had been selling her innocence to the highest bidder, disappeared again when her husband's money came with strings attached, disappeared completely when her father died and left her with nothing but bad memories and Hans the German shepherd.

Each disappearance had taught her something new about survival. How to look pitiable when you had money. How to seem simple when you were calculating every move. How to appear helpless when you had a loaded pistol in your purse and knew exactly how to use it.

She'd practiced disappearing in that shack, target shooting at bottles lined up on driftwood, perfecting her aim the way she'd perfected everything else. The airport wanted her land, and she'd sell it to them, but first she'd erase every trace of who she'd been there.

The duck boat bobbed at the dock—Whitey's boat that would never carry him hunting again. She couldn't bear to sell it, couldn't bear to keep it. So she'd leave it for whoever found it, another piece of someone else's life floating free.

Walking to her car for the last time, Wally ran her hand along the spare tire mounted on the fender. She'd kept that spare through the war when tires were being confiscated, another small victory in a life built on staying one step ahead of anyone who might take something from her.

The real secret wasn't that she'd been a Ziegfeld girl or married money or learned to shoot straight. The real secret was that she'd mastered the most important skill of all: how to become invisible while hiding in plain sight.

As she drove away from the shack, past the "Private Property" sign that had kept the world at bay, Wally carried with her the knowledge that some secrets are meant to be kept forever. Some secrets are meant to be buried under airport runways, sealed beneath concrete where no one can ever dig them up again.

The butcher's daughter, the chorus girl, the banker's wife, the eccentric recluse—all of them had been Wally, and none of them had been real. The real Wilhelmina Krause had learned to disappear so completely that even she couldn't find herself anymore.

And maybe that was the point. Maybe the greatest secret of all was knowing when to let go of who you used to be and become someone else entirely, someone who could survive whatever came next.

The sun set behind her as she drove toward the boarding house, toward her small room with its hotplate and chair by the window. Toward the final act of a woman who'd learned that the best way to keep a secret was to become one yourself.

Chapter 9: One Vacation

The chicken farm was the only vacation we'd ever have, and it came with a price I didn't know I'd have to pay. Uncle Charlie made that clear from the first morning when he handed me the wire basket at six o'clock.

"Time to collect eggs," he said, not bothering to wake my cousin Susan, who had perfected the art of refusing to do anything. I was free labor, and we both knew it.

I loved slipping my hand under the warm hens' bodies, stealing their eggs like a thief in the night. The hens would sit there, not even blinking, as I liberated what they'd dropped without a thought. No motherly instinct lived in their hearts—eggs were just something that fell out of them, like chicken poop.

My aunt took me down to the basement to do a DIY on candling the eggs, holding each one up to the bright light to check for dark spots that meant life was beginning inside. How an egg could ever have a dark spot when there were no roosters in the entire flock was a question I kept to myself, but she did explain it to me without my questioning. We worked quietly, as though we were in a sacred place, looking for the miracle of creation in a simple white orb.

"The spots would mean a rooster got into the flock," she explained, her voice soft as always. But roosters were forbidden on an egg farm—they were gathered up early and sold to someone else who needed them. Brought to the farm in small boxes of 100 there was no way initially to know which one might be a rooster until a little bit longer.

The secret was that everything on the farm had its purpose, and when that purpose ended, so did the creature. I learned this the day Uncle Charlie decided to show me how to eliminate old hens from his flock.

"When hens get old, about three years old, they're not good layers anymore," he said, cornering a hen that had been laying shell-less eggs—soft, leather-like sacks that couldn't be sold.

I watched in frozen horror as he grabbed the old hen by the neck. "You have to wring its neck so it's easier to manage."

The clucking stopped suddenly with a small, terrible sound. The other hens began screaming, running around in a whirl of white feathers, but he wasn't finished.

"It's not hard to do. Anyone can do it," he said, as though teaching me to change a tire. I do not want to see or learn this lesson.

My mind screamed, "Run!" but my legs wouldn't carry me away. Something sick and hot came over me as he reached for the small hatchet near the tree stump.

"From here, you have an easier job." He raised the hatchet and brought it down with a single blow.

But the headless hen didn't fall. It began running around the yard, spurting blood everywhere as I pressed myself against the fence, praying to disappear into the wood. I'd never seen so much blood in my life. I was feeling nauseous and paralyzed.

Why did he have to show me that? I had no intention of killing hens. I knew we ate chickens and knew someone had to kill them, but did I have to see it? Was this supposed to be my passage to adulthood?

I'd already learned about death when my father died. I didn't need another lesson delivered in blood and feathers.

The secret Uncle Charlie was really teaching me wasn't about chicken farming. It was about the casual cruelty that men like him carried inside, the way they could watch something suffer and call it education. Just like my father had done with the hot spoon on my hand, just like Uncle Charlie did to my aunt at dinnertime, finding small excuses to belittle her.

But there were other secrets on that farm, gentler ones. My aunt teaching me to make farmer cheese in the blazing sun, the striped pillowcase ticking hanging from the clothesline like a strange flag of surrender. Her hands moving through tatting without looking, creating intricate flowers from thread and patience. My aunt was a woman who knew that work was necessary, and she worked on the farm in addition to a job she had.

She was paid in silver dollars by the coat factory—twenty dollars a week for sewing linings into expensive women's coats. No benefits, no sick days, just piecework that kept the failing farm barely afloat. She'd die ten years later of a massive heart attack at fifty-two, her heart worn out from carrying too much weight.

The real secret of our only vacation was that it wasn't a vacation at all. It was an education in how people survive when the world offers them nothing but hard choices. How my aunt endured Uncle Charlie's anger. How the coat factory women accepted whatever pay they were given. How old hens paid the price for no longer being useful.

That night, sitting on the screened porch with my mother and aunt, watching fireflies blink like tiny lanterns in the darkness, I understood something about the different kinds of secrets families keep. Some protect you from knowing too much too soon. Others prepare you for a world that doesn't care whether you're ready or not. I'd learn much later in life that one of their secrets was never intended to be discovered. Their father, my grandfather, had been arrested for horse theft in Brooklyn and sent to prison. For that reason, my mother, the oldest of the four children, had to quit elementary school and go to work in an artificial flower factory. It was their collective secret shame.

The headless chicken running through that yard had been my introduction to the secret that survival often requires watching terrible things happen and calling them necessary. That sometimes the people who are supposed to protect you are the ones who hurt you casually.

But sitting there in the peaceful darkness, listening to crickets and watching my aunt's hands create beauty from thread, I learned another secret: that grace can exist alongside cruelty, that gentleness can survive in the hardest places, and that sometimes the most important lessons come not from what people teach you, but from what they show you about who you never want to become. Uncle Charlie was a man capable of extreme rage, but I never knew it, and I never even suspected it that day when the hen met her fatal end.

The farm would fail again, just like the first one. Uncle Charlie would move on as a Class A mechanic to fix Cadillacs in some upscale town. But I would carry both secrets with me—the one written in blood and the one whispered in twilight conversations between women who understood that survival sometimes looks like sitting quietly in rocking chairs, creating something beautiful while the world falls apart around you.

Chapter 10: The Movie Theatres

"Children have to sit in the children's section," the matron in the black dress with the white collar said, pointing toward the seats right in front of the screen. We'd crane our necks back like spectators at a tennis match, heads swinging side to side to follow the action, but we didn't care. For fifteen cents, we had access to heaven.

The secret wasn't just getting into this particular theater—it was staying there all day despite the matrons with their flashlights, prowling the aisles like prison guards looking for contraband children. Horrific visions flash through our heads if we were to be caught.

Even the entrance into the theater, when you didn't have money, posed a particular type of collusion. But today, I had fifteen cents.

"No, stay back here against the wall in front of the posters," Cosmo whispered as the crowd surged toward the box office.

"Why? I have to buy a ticket."

"You can get in without buying a ticket and you know it. If we rush up with the whole crowd, we'll get in for free." His disgusted look said everything about what he thought of girls who followed rules.

But I couldn't stomach the risk. I bought my ticket and watched from the corner of my eye as his plan unfolded. The raucous crowd charged forward in one enormous surge, overwhelming the ticket taker, who raised his hands helplessly.

"Wait, wait, let me take your ticket! Stop and form a line!" It was all in vain, and he knew it.

The solid wave of children had already overwhelmed him, and I saw Cosmo slip along the wall like a shadow, disappearing into the theater without paying. The ticket taker fumbled with stubs stuck in his face while half the kids slithered past him for free.

That was the first secret—how to become invisible in plain sight, how to use chaos as camouflage. But the real artistry came later, when the matrons began their hunt.

After the cartoons and serials ended, they'd stalk the aisles with their flashlights, ordering all children to leave. The house lights never came on—they preferred to work in the darkness, their beacons sweeping across seats like searchlights at a prison.

"Look out, watch out!" Tommy pushed against me as we squeezed down between the seats, surrounded by popcorn boxes and empty soda cups. The rough fabric brushed unpleasantly against our faces as we buried ourselves in the debris of other people's entertainment.

"Watch out. She'll see us!"

"Shut up. She'll hear you," I whispered, giving him a strong push.

I could see her flashlight dipping into the seats, working methodically down each row. Her black laced shoes passed by our hiding spot, the yellow beam flashing above us like a lighthouse that had missed our ship.

Safe. For now.

We'd wait fifteen minutes for the matrons to go off duty, then squirm across the center aisle into the adult section where we could watch the double feature all over again. The theater was our refuge from the heat, our air-conditioned sanctuary in a world that offered few comforts to children with fifteen cents and nowhere else to go.

But my favorite theater wasn't the this one with its forgiving ticket takers and easy hiding spots. It was the Loew's movie palace, where stepping onto the thick carpet felt like entering another world entirely.

Huge mirrors lined the walls, brass rails separated the entrance into three discrete paths, and ushers in gold-buttoned uniforms stood at attention like palace guards. A massive goldfish pond greeted you at the base of steps leading to the loge seats—luxury tickets at a dollar twenty-five that were impossibly out of reach for kids like us.

The ceiling was painted to look like an open Roman amphitheater, complete with blue sky, clouds, and twinkling stars. For twenty-five cents, you could sit under artificial heaven and forget you were poor.

But the matrons at Loew's were different—more starched women in black dresses with white collars who seemed imported from some authoritarian nightmare. They were taller, more efficient, impossible to escape.

"You, kid, get up and get out! No children in the evening shows!"

Their harsh voices cut through the darkness like commands from drill sergeants. They never missed us, never gave us a chance to disappear into the seats or slip past their vigilant watch.

"And take those candy boxes with you! You know you're not allowed in the Adult Section!"

The real secret wasn't about sneaking into movies or hiding from matrons. It was about understanding the invisible lines that divided the world—who belonged where, who could afford what, who got to stay, and who got thrown out.

The loge seats at Loew's weren't just more expensive; they were a different species of comfort entirely. They reclined like living room chairs, covered in wonderful fabric that made you feel rich just by touching it. I sat there once and gloried in it, understanding for the first time what money could actually buy.

Down the street, The Savoy sent desperate ushers running to steal customers with promises of twelve cartoons instead of ten, nickel sodas, and no one chasing you out at noon. But none of us budged. We knew the difference between a palace and a dump, between first-run films and whatever desperate programming The Savoy could afford. It was a dump, and we knew it. Everybody passed the word around.

The secret was that we were training ourselves to want more—more comfort, more beauty, more respect. Every time we squeezed under those theater seats to avoid the matrons, every time we pressed our faces against the velvet ropes separating us from the loge section, we were learning the geography of class and privilege.

We were poor kids with fifteen cents buying temporary citizenship in worlds that would normally exclude us. But we were also learning the art of escape—not just from hot summer streets, but from the assumption that people like us didn't deserve better.

In the darkness of those theaters, surrounded by the magic of moving pictures and air conditioning, we were secretly practicing for the lives we'd build later. Learning to recognize quality when we saw it, learning to slip past barriers that seemed insurmountable, learning that sometimes the best way to belong somewhere is simply to refuse to leave.

The matrons with their flashlights never understood what they were really hunting. They thought they were chasing children out of adult spaces. But we were the future, hiding in plain sight, already planning our return. We'd begun to understand the power of hiding and the secrets that needed to be kept in order to enter those sacred spaces we craved.

Chapter 11: The Taste of Memory

The frozen peas and carrots on the stranger's plate stopped me cold on that Manhattan sidewalk. Orange chunks and too-green pearls—like tiny jewels scattered across white porcelain, innocent as childhood but sharp as broken glass in my chest.

My expensive heels clicked against the pavement as I stood there, a woman in a wool coat with possum trim, looking every inch the successful magazine editor I'd become. But those vegetables? They dragged me back to linoleum floors and the smell of fish trucks, to a time when frozen food was magic and secrets lived in closets like monsters under the bed.

"Want to drive?" my brother would ask, and I always said yes. Who wouldn't? At six, the possibility of control feels like magic. You don't understand yet that some wheels can't be steered, some brakes don't work, some crashes are inevitable.

The truck smelled awful from those wet, fishy papers, but I loved it anyway. Hot damn, it was glorious! That's what I told myself as we lurched around the lot, him turning white every time I nearly clipped a car. I was fearless then, riding running boards and hanging off trucks, pulling myself up just before the wheels could claim me. Yes, this was where my dad worked as a parking lot attendant in a lot owned by the mafia.

I almost didn't make it out of the wheels' way, but I never told him. Some truths are too heavy for others to carry. Besides, he'd stop letting me hang onto the truck's side as he practiced driving in the lot.

Years later, I'd drive his coupe on Long Island roads, forgetting to brake on turns, spinning like characters escaping from the Keystone Cops. He'd scream, "Off the gas! Off the gas!" but I couldn't stop. I'd learned to drive forward at any cost, even when the world was spinning out of control.

I was six again, sitting on my brother's lap in Sam's Fish Market delivery truck. No doors, no keys needed, just bloody newspapers in the back and the acrid smell of yesterday's catch. He taught me to drive in that parking lot next to our house—me working the stick shift while he handled the clutch my short legs couldn't reach.

"Smooth," he'd say, "don't jerk it. Look ahead, not down."

But I always looked down. At the gearshift rising from bare metal like a small broom handle. My hands were too small for the work they were trying to do. I was amazed at everything except what was coming.

The fish truck was freedom, but freedom has a price. Every secret does.

Certain foods now would always bring me back to memories I didn't want and secrets I had to keep. Standing there on that busy street, watching office workers rush past in their perfect lives, I remembered the day everything changed. The day the red spread across our white bathroom tiles like tiny rivers reaching toward the walls was unforgettable. That was the day I learned that some stains never wash out, no matter how hard you scrub.

My mother was making potato pancakes that evening. I can still see the raw ingredients in that heavy brown bowl with its thin decorative ring—the only bowl we owned that wasn't chipped or given to us piece by piece from dish night at the movies. We never completed a set of anything in our house. Not dishes, not families, not safety.

The bowl sat on our metal kitchen table with its oilcloth covering, surrounded by the collection of mismatched china we'd gathered from summer homes and cleaning jobs. Each cup and saucer told a story of someone else's abundance, someone else's wholeness. We lived in the spaces between their plenty.

I had one treasure—a china cup with fluted sides, aqua blue and gold with delicate curves. Too beautiful to use, too precious to risk. I kept it on the highest shelf where it couldn't be broken, where it stayed perfect and untouchable. Like the truth.

The memories played like broken film in my mind—scenes I could edit and rearrange but never truly escape. I was the projectionist and the audience, the star and the critic, keeping it all in repair for a show that never ended.

Standing on that Manhattan street in my expensive heels and designer "sale" woolen coat, I was everything I'd never been allowed to dream of becoming. College graduate (a lie). Successful career woman (half true). Someone who shopped at Bloomingdale's and used a tortoise shell cigarette holder (absolutely true, and absolutely armor).

The perfect product of middle-American society, except for the movies playing behind my gray eyes. The ones where red rivers flow across bathroom white tiles. Where children hide in closets, learning that some doors should never be opened. Where potato pancakes represent the last normal dinnertime before everything breaks apart.

I'd buried my Queens accent under careful pauses and designer clothes. I'd buried the girl who drove a fish truck and rode running boards. I'd buried the truth so deep that sometimes I forgot it myself.

But peas and carrots remember everything.

That china cup with the fluted edges? Lost in a fire that claimed more than dishes. Gone with the house and the secrets and the childhood that ended too soon. But not forgotten. Never forgotten.

The businessman finished his lunch and left. I straightened my collar and continued walking toward Grand Central, each step taking me further from Queens and closer to the woman I'd built myself to be.

Behind me, in the luncheonette window, new plates appeared with new combinations of food. Other people's comfort, other people's memories, other people's ordinary moments that would never haunt them in Manhattan traffic.

I walked on, carrying my beautiful burden of broken film and borrowed china, of fish trucks and frozen food, of the day the red rivers flowed and childhood learned to hide in closets.

Some secrets are too powerful to stay buried. They wait in vegetables and memories, in the taste of poverty and the smell of fish, ready to rise like ghosts when you least expect them.

I never wanted to be poor again. But I'd learned something more important: I never wanted to be that afraid again, hiding in closets while the world fell apart upstairs.

The city swallowed me back into its rhythm, but I carried Queens with me—all its rough magic and beautiful disasters, all its lessons about survival and the price of dreams.

Some stains never wash out. But sometimes, that's exactly the point.

Chapter 12: My Unfortunate Birth

The straight pins holding Sister Margaret's habit together caught the morning light as she bent to lift the wicker basket. Seven-year-old Mary Catherine pressed her belly deeper into the sandy dirt beneath the convent hedges, Tommy beside her breathing so loud she was sure the nun would hear.

"Stay down," she whispered, tasting grit on her lower lip.

They'd been planning this reconnaissance mission for weeks. What did nuns wear under those enormous black outfits? The question plagued every kid in the parish, but no adult would tell them. Some secrets, Mary Catherine had learned, you had to steal.

Sister Margaret stepped into the garden, wooden clothespins already between her teeth. The laundry basket settled at her feet with a soft thud. Mary Catherine's heart hammered against the ground as the first white garment emerged.

"Holy cow," Tommy breathed beside her.

The "bras" looked like baby belly bands, designed to flatten whatever curves God might have blessed the nuns with. No wonder they looked like walking boards under those habits. Next came enormous white bloomers that billowed in the June breeze like small parachutes, and undershirts that could have fit her father.

"Where are the regular lady things?" Tommy whispered.

Mary Catherine didn't answer. She was thinking about her mother's delicate undergarments hanging on their line at home, so different from these institutional white tents. Her mother, who'd tried to kill herself and the baby that would become Mary Catherine. Her mother, who now slept in a separate bedroom from her father. Her mother, whose own secrets ran deeper than what she wore beneath her housedresses.

Sister Margaret paused, clothespin suspended in midair. Her head turned toward the hedge, squinting against the morning sun. Mary Catherine held her breath until her lungs burned. The nun's gaze swept the perimeter of the garden, searching for whatever instinct told her was watching.

Nothing. Sister Margaret returned to her laundry.

Mary Catherine thought about secrets then, pressed into the dirt with her friend, stealing glimpses of nuns' underwear. How the biggest secrets weren't the ones you discovered by hiding in hedges. The biggest secrets lived in kitchen ovens and separate bedrooms, in the space between what adults said and what they meant.

"She won't live past her sixth month," the doctor had said about Mary Catherine, according to family lore. But here she was, seven years old and learning that some mysteries weren't worth solving. The nuns' underwear was just cloth, after all. Practical and plain and nothing like the secrets that actually mattered.

Sister Margaret hung the last petticoat and gathered her empty basket. As her black habit disappeared through the kitchen door, Mary Catherine and Tommy crawled backward through the hedge opening, emerging grass-stained and triumphant on the school side of the fence.

"Wait until I tell everyone," Tommy said, brushing dirt from his knees.

But Mary Catherine was quiet, thinking about her mother's face that morning when she'd asked where babies came from. The way her mother's eyes had gone somewhere else entirely before she'd said, "God just blesses women, dear."

Some secrets, Mary Catherine realized, were kept not because they were shameful, but because they were too heavy for small shoulders. Like the secret of nearly dying before you were born. Like the secret of being unwanted until your father saved you both from an oven full of gas.

Walking home past the cemetery where she sometimes picked bouquets for her mother, Mary Catherine decided she wouldn't tell anyone about the nun's underwear. Let the other kids wonder. Let them create their own mysteries to solve.

She had bigger secrets to carry now. Secrets about mothers who used golden caps instead of rhythm methods. Secrets about fathers who slept alone. Secrets about survival that had nothing to do with what anyone wore beneath their clothes.

The Rose-of-Sharon was blooming outside their kitchen window when she got home, the same flowers her mother had seen when her father pulled her from the oven. Mary Catherine stopped to smell them, understanding suddenly that some secrets weren't meant to be stolen or solved.

Some secrets were lived with, like slightly shorter arms and the knowledge that you almost weren't here at all. Like knowing your mother had wanted to die rather than have you, and that your father's love had been strong enough to save you both.

The laundry on their line fluttered in the afternoon breeze—her mother's delicate things and her father's work clothes, hanging separate but sharing the same clothesline. Mary Catherine went inside to tell her mother she was home from school, carrying the weight of new secrets and old truths, learning that the most important mysteries weren't hidden under habits at all.

Chapter 13: The Butcher

The Butcher hobbled down the alley on his single crutch, his artificial leg hidden somewhere in his meager possessions while his pants leg was rolled up and pinned to his knee with a safety pin. I watched from our back step as he made his way toward the Avenue, hat ready for the day's performance.

"Here, kid," he said, stretching out his one free arm with three nickels in his palm. "Go see a picture show."

My mother didn't like me taking money from any of the Bottle Babies, but fifteen cents meant heaven to me—a ticket to the movies and escape from the alley's harsh realities. The Butcher knew I never got an allowance, knew I survived on the nickels I could get from returning deposit bottles I collected in the corners where the drunks had tossed them.

"I told you I don't want you to go near that man. Do you hear me?" Her voice carried a sharp edge that meant business.

I heard her, but like so many other things I heard, I didn't always follow instructions.

The Butcher was the antithesis of Rube—the darkest of the Bottle Babies, next to Mossy. I always assumed he'd gotten his nickname because he carried a knife hidden somewhere in his clothes. Never knew for certain, but something in his eyes suggested violence simmered just beneath the surface, ready to slice through whatever stood in his way.

He was pure theater on the Avenue. The missing leg, the dirty crutch, the sometimes eye patch when he deemed it appropriate—all props in his daily performance. Who would pass up a man with half a leg asking politely for money? But I'd seen him when the mood shifted, when politeness dissolved into something nasty as hell.

The fights between him and Mossy were legendary. They'd battle over Sneaky Pete that Mossy refused to share, over the Mulligan Stew that might contain an extra piece of meat, over cardboard territory that meant the difference between shelter and sleeping exposed to the elements.

Where The Butcher slept remained a mystery to me until I noticed the rustling under boxes on the loading dock at the end of the alley. The toy store's concrete platform held a pile of cardboard arranged away from the elevator doors, and sometimes in the early morning, as the sun crept across the gravel, those boxes would move ever so slightly.

The mechanics from the car repair shop had learned to keep their eyes fixed straight ahead as they walked past. They treated The Butcher and Mossy like the huge tomcats that roamed the area—there, but to be avoided at all costs. A kind word would bring recriminations and splashes of tobacco spit aimed at their fresh coveralls.

But I began to understand something the adults around me knew instinctively: the Bottle Babies served a purpose beyond their own survival. Who would dare disturb a surly, filthy, drunken man sleeping in a cardboard box to steal from the stores behind him? The Butcher and his kind were unwitting watchdogs, their reputation for unpredictability keeping thieves away more effectively than any security system.

The store owners understood this arrangement. A dollar here and there was a small price to pay for protection that never asked for a contract or demanded regular payments. It wasn't exactly protection money—this neighborhood was off-limits to those kinds of operations. The local mobsters in the bar saw to that. It was a simple win-win situation disguised as charity.

Jimmy was different from the others—thin, Irish, always quivering from either alcohol withdrawal or anxiety attacks. He was the only Bottle Baby permitted to enter our backyard, and his arrival was always announced by the gentle sound of the gate latch opening.

He'd knock on our back door and speak in a low voice: "Mrs., do you have anything extra to eat?"

Though our door was never locked, he waited for my mother to respond. She'd disappear into the kitchen and return with two bologna sandwiches wrapped in wax paper, placed carefully in a small paper bag for his dignity.

"Thank you, Mrs.," he'd say, stuffing the bag into his jacket pocket before walking away up the alley, ashes crunching under his feet.

Those ashes were our early warning system. The alley was wide enough for a car and open to all, but no one used it as a shortcut between our street and the Avenue. Footsteps on ashes meant someone was coming—and strangers could mean danger to a house full of women, especially after my father died.

One afternoon, I watched The Butcher attempt to share Mossy's cardboard territory. The result was swift and violent—a rock sailed through the air, missing The Butcher's head by inches as Mossy's voice carried across the alley in a stream of curses that made the mechanics quicken their pace.

That's when I realized the brutal mathematics of their existence. Comfort had to be found at a safe distance from Mossy, and that was an unbroken rule among the Bottle Babies. The Butcher would have to find Jimmy or another of the weaker men, intimidate them enough to share their cardboard, or spend the night exposed to whatever weather came.

The secret I learned from watching The Butcher wasn't about generosity or kindness—his occasional nickels came with the understanding that someday I might be useful to him. It was about survival in a world where human dignity had been stripped away, leaving only the raw mechanics of getting through another day.

But there was something else, something the adults understood and I was just beginning to grasp: even in their broken state, these men maintained their own code. Jimmy never tried to open our unlocked door. The Butcher never asked for more than what was freely given. They respected boundaries even when society had stopped respecting theirs.

Years later, I would understand that The Butcher taught me my first lesson about the complexity of human nature—that people could be both generous and manipulative, both pitiable and dangerous, both victims and survivors. That sometimes the most broken among us still follow rules invisible to those who've never had to fight for cardboard and crust.

The real secret wasn't in the nickels he gave me or the performances he put on for strangers. It was in learning that survival creates its own morality, and that compassion and caution aren't opposites—they're necessary partners in a world where kindness can be both salvation and vulnerability.

Chapter 14: A Kitchen Caboose

The scratching in the walls started our first night in the hundred-year-old farmhouse, but my father said not to worry—he'd take care of it. The house had radiators instead of the hot bricks wrapped in flannel that had warmed my bed in our cold-water flat. Progress, my mother called it, though she didn't mention the rats that came with the upgrade.

"Steel wool and broken glass," my father explained, stuffing the mixture into cracks around the radiators. "If you can't afford an exterminator, you use the old-fashioned method."

But some rats were too clever for steel wool. That's when the actual battle began in the basement, with metal traps and the terrible sounds of my father fighting them in semi-darkness. The crack of skulls against stone walls—thump, thump, thump—then silence. He'd emerge with a burlap sack, disappearing up the alley to dispose of evidence I never wanted to see.

The house kept its own secrets. Built by farmers when our town was potato fields, it had grown like Topsy—rooms tacked on without architectural plan, just muscle power and wooden framing. The kitchen stepped down from the rest of the house, an afterthought addition. But the strangest feature was the half-caboose attached, like a railroad car that had lost its way and decided to stay.

Inside the caboose, an old well opening still gaped, its water bucket hanging like a reminder of harder times. The small window and steel hand bars revealed its origin, painted now to match the house but fooling no one about what it really was.

The dining room held the house's one touch of elegance—an enormous oak table with lion's claw feet that took my breath away. I'd never seen anything so beautiful, carved with incredible detail that spoke of money we'd never have. It stood like a magnificent symbol of someplace far from where we lived on the social ladder, smelling of dreams that belonged to other people. It wasn't the dining room table that snagged my complete attention, but a small radio.

My refuge was my small Crosley positioned on a two-shelf table, where I'd listen to "Let's Pretend" and "The Shadow" on Saturday mornings. When it broke, the yellow glow disappearing from the dial, my world nearly ended. Mr. Stevens down the street fixed it for twenty-five cents—a quarter that meant everything when fairy tales hung in the balance.

"Don't worry, dolly," my mother said, using the name she saved for my near-death experiences. "Mr. Stevens can fix radios."

The Stevens family lived on Home Relief, enduring monthly visits from a social worker who demanded coffee and cake from people who watered down milk for their children. My father would never apply for such assistance—he felt it was an indignity that meant he couldn't provide for his family, He turned to the mafia, and they provided.

But the real secret of the house was upstairs, behind the sealed door that led to the adjoining apartment where the landlady's sister lived alone. Annie was a small, frail woman with glasses so thick her eyes looked enormous, sentenced to isolation in one room while her sister controlled her inheritance and threatened to return her to the psychiatric hospital.

The scratching I heard wasn't always rats. Sometimes it was Annie, trying to find her way through darkness with her impaired vision, her fingernails seeking safety on walls and doors in a world that had forgotten her existence.

I avoided the second floor, especially at bedtime, convinced that the woman behind the sealed door was an axe murderer instead of what she really was—another victim of circumstances beyond her control. The seal was just tape, after all. How could that hold if someone really wanted to get through?

When I couldn't bear the fear upstairs, I'd find other refuges. The huge tree with heart-shaped leaves became my respite from everything human, a place to sit quietly above the world's chaos. Or I'd climb to the top shelf of the downstairs coat closet, curling up alone in that dark, warm space where peace lived in the silence.

"Is she all right? She just sits there," my Aunt Mary would ask, watching me seek solitude.

But my mother never seemed surprised to find me hiding. Maybe she understood that some children need small spaces to contain the largeness of what they're trying to process—the scratching in walls, the secrets behind sealed doors, the way adults carried pain that leaked into every room of a house.

The kitchen caboose held the secret of adaptability—how farmers had made do with whatever they could get, sawing train cars in half and turning them into pantries. Not artistic, but inventive. Survivors who understood that sometimes the strangest solutions are the ones that work.

Later, when the house burned down and we moved again, I'd carry with me the knowledge learned in those small spaces—that sanctuary can be found anywhere you can fit yourself, that some scratching comes from creatures trying to survive, and that the most beautiful furniture in the world can't mask the tensions that live in the spaces between rooms.

The secret wasn't about the rats or the sealed doors or even the woman who lived behind them. It was about learning that survival sometimes means making yourself small enough to hide in coat closets and high enough to climb trees, finding peace in radio programs and safety in spaces designed for one.

Chapter 15: A Blue Suit Day

The hospital hallway was darker than I remembered, empty except for the tired man in rumpled whites who emerged from the shadows to speak with my mother. I watched from what felt like the wrong end of a telescope as she stood bathed in dull yellow light, her voice too low to hear.

My shoes squeaked on the linoleum as we walked back to the elevators. The only sound in all that silence.

On the bus home, my mother stared straight ahead and fished for her house keys two blocks early. She held them like a weapon, ready to jab at anyone who might attack us. It was a ritual I'd see for years to come. She learned to do that when she was almost mugged coming home from a part-time hospital shift late at night.

"Your father is dead," she said after we passed the anemic shrub and entered our hundred-year-old house.

The funeral director asked for payment before they'd discuss where the body would go. My mother handed over the envelope from the dresser drawer—a thousand dollars my father had saved for this exact moment. No insurance, just discipline and the knowledge that death comes for working men without warning.

They dressed him in his navy-blue suit with the pink shirt he loved. I'd never seen him wear a suit before, but death required formality he'd never needed in life. His hands were clasped across his chest, the scar from his skin cancer hidden by careful positioning and makeup that changed his orange-colored face to something more natural. He was gone now, and we'd never know if he really had kidnapped a member of British royalty for a night on the town with his friends. Yes, he'd claimed it was the Duke of Windsor.

The flowers had a scent all their own—not like the roses I picked in the cemetery, but heavy with the weight of endings. I knelt beside my mother, said a prayer, and that was it. I would never see his face again. Photo album. We had only one photo of him clowning in my brother's elementary school graduation outfit. Another one taken in France when he was in the army, with a snake around his neck, would be destroyed by my mother in a fit of depression.

At the funeral mass, they made me sit with my class instead of my family. The entire school had been marched over to witness my father's send-off, his coffin draped with an American flag at the altar. Why wasn't I sitting with my mother and grandfather? Whose decision was that?

The real secret came later, when everyone else had gone home.

My brother had to stay behind at the funeral parlor for a ritual I didn't know existed. When a man died, his oldest son—and my father only had one—would be given a heavy hammer and six long spikes. It was his job to nail the coffin shut for eternity.

I can only imagine what that felt like. All those dinner table arguments that ended with my father's taunt: "You'll be pushing up daisies before me." All those times my brother would yell back, "No, you will."

The weight lifting and boxing with friends, maybe preparing for a fight that would never come the way he'd imagined.

"Take these nails one by one," the funeral director would have said, "and put them where I say."

The first nail went above my father's head. The hammer bounced back—not hard enough. "You have to hit it harder. This wood is strong."

Six times my brother would raise that hammer, using every muscle he'd built, bringing it down with his full body weight behind it. Six spikes for all those years of taunts. Not exactly sufficient payback, but something.

The sound would have echoed through the empty room. Bam! Each blow carrying the weight of every harsh word, every dinner eaten in tense silence, every promise that one of them would die first.

When it was finished, he handed back the hammer without a final prayer or goodbye. Just done.

The rest happened quickly. The Plymouth sedan with its trunk full of quality tools sold for fifty dollars to a man who knew exactly what he was stealing from a desperate widow. "Considering you're a recent widow and all," he'd said, pocketing keys to a car worth twenty times what he paid.

The tools my father had loaned to neighbors disappeared without a trace. The duck hunting boat, the outboard motor—all gone so fast you barely remembered they'd existed.

But the real secret wasn't in the missing possessions or the funeral rituals or even the insurance salesman who'd tried to sell my mother policies on her children's lives. The secret was in the hammer's weight, in my brother's muscles finally finding their purpose, in the way grief can look like revenge when it's really just the end of waiting for something that will never come.

Death had settled the argument about who would push up daisies first. But it hadn't settled anything about the weight we carry afterward—the guilt of relief, the shame of survival, the way love and hatred can share the same space in a son's heart as he seals his father into darkness.

Some secrets live in the space between the hammer's rise and fall, in the moment when justice and duty become the same thing, when the only way to honor a father is to make sure he can never hurt you again.

The funeral was over. The blue suit day was done. And somewhere in a cemetery on Long Island, my father waited in his wooden box, sealed tight by the hands of the son who'd finally won their last argument.

Chapter 16: After the Funeral

Click knew something was wrong when my mother put his harness on. His graying muzzle lifted toward her face, brown eyes searching for the truth we were all trying to hide. The dog had belonged to my father, sleeping at the foot of his bed every night for fifteen years, and now my father was gone.

"He has to go," my mother said, her voice as flat as concrete. "He's too sick." Vets' bills weren't in any budget we'd have now that Daddy was gone, and our only hope was a slender, very anxious girl quitting high school and entering the unknown world of "business," as my mother said. For her, it was terrifying; for us, it was a life raft in a sea of uncertainty.

We all knew what that meant. The trip down the hill past the railroad trestle to the ASPCA, where dogs went in alive and came out in a pile behind the building. I'd seen that pile once—fur coats stacked on top of each other until you got close enough to see the paws, the legs, the unmistakable shapes of bodies waiting for the garbage truck.

I ran my hand over Click's rough, mottled coat one last time, feeling the warmth of his skin through the fur. He'd let me tumble him into my baby carriage when I was small, never complained, never tried to jump out. He just went along with whatever game I wanted to play, his face wearing that expression I'd learned to love—the one that looked like a smile.

"I can't watch," I whispered.

None of us could. We accused my mother of being cruel and heartless, but she was doing the only thing possible. There was no money for veterinarians, no choice but the last walk down that hill.

Click didn't know where he was going. He trusted us completely, taking each gingerly step in his harness, looking straight ahead as my mother led him out the door. The thud of that door closing was the last sound of his life in our house.

Forty-five minutes later, she returned without the harness and leash. The deed was done. Another door in our lives had closed—first Daddy, now his dog.

But secrets have a way of revealing themselves when you least expect them. As they say, "When one door closes, another opens."

"I love him, but I can't keep him," the man said, standing in our yard with his eyes cast downward. "I'm living in a rooming house, and they won't allow dogs."

Beside him sat the most magnificent animal I'd ever seen. Black and brown, powerfully built, muscles packed and ready to spring into action. Louie was a war dog, a K-9 trained to kill on command. His handler had brought him back from the war, but now he needed a home.

"You don't have any men in your home anymore," the man continued. "You live only with your daughters. You need someone to protect you, and Louie would fit the bill perfectly."

The secret was that some losses prepare you for unexpected gifts. Click's death had left a hole in our defenses, and now this trained killer was being offered to fill it. Not just a pet, but a bodyguard who could crush a man's throat with his enormous jaws if given the signal.

Louie was nothing like our gentle Click. When strangers approached, the ridge of hair along his back would rise, and he'd bare fangs that could end a life in seconds. But with us, he was obedient, controlled, waiting for commands that we prayed we'd never have to give.

The real secret was simpler than any of us understood then: sometimes protection comes disguised as loss. Click's death seemed like another cruelty in a year full of them, but it opened the space for Louie to enter our lives just when we needed him most.

I learned this watching from my hiding spot across from the vaudeville theater, standing on my metal skates in the shadows of the auto repair shop. Through the open dressing room windows, I could see cowboys in silky outfits preparing for their show—Roy Rogers and his troupe getting ready to perform.

I couldn't afford the three-dollar ticket to see the show, but I could watch from the shadows. That's where most of my life happened anyway—in the spaces between what I could have and what I could see, between loss and unexpected grace.

My sister understood. Somehow she'd saved enough money to buy me those red leather cowboy boots I'd been staring at in the shoe store window. They pinched my toes something awful, but I never complained. She'd denied herself things for months to save up that money, and her gift was worth more than comfort.

That was the secret about protection and love. Not just from trained war dogs or punch-drunk fighters who hung around the bookies, but from sisters who noticed what you wanted and found ways to give it to you. From mothers who made the hard choices so you didn't have to. From dogs who trusted you even when you were leading them to cross the rainbow bridge.

Click never looked back as he walked down that hill. He believed we were taking him somewhere good, and maybe we were. Maybe the last walk is just another kind of gift when staying means suffering. And he would have suffered.

Louie sat by my side now, alert and ready, his keen brown eyes watching for threats I couldn't even imagine. He was the secret that emerged from our sorrow—protection born from loss, strength that came only after we'd been broken.

Some endings are really beginnings wearing disguises we don't recognize until much later, when we're safe enough to look back and understand what actually saved us.

Chapter 17: The Price of Protection

The "Flats Fixed" sign went up on our barn on a Tuesday (yes, we had a barn in our backyard) and by Wednesday everyone in the neighborhood knew what it really meant. Not that anyone would say it out loud—some secrets are too dangerous to speak, even when everyone knows them.

Big Al had approached our landlady with dollar signs dancing in his eyes. One hundred dollars a month for the use of our sagging barn, no questions asked. May practically genuflected when he made the offer. Who was going to rent an old barn, anyway?

I learned about bribes from my hiding spot behind the lace curtains, watching the horse cop lean down toward Lefty in the alley. The conversation looked casual enough—two men shaking hands—but I saw the roll of twenties pass between them like communion wafers.

"Hey, what's the matter with you?" Lefty kept smiling, his voice all honey and reason. "Didn't I say we'd take care of you? Haven't we always taken care of you guys?"

The cop's face transformed from scowl to a grin the moment those bills touched his palm. "Yeah, I knew you were good for it, but someone at the station said they'd been stiffed the other day."

"Nah, no problem. We're good. See you next week, same time."

That was how the world really worked—not the way they taught us in school about law and order, but through handshakes that carried more weight than any judge's gavel. The secret was that everyone had their price, and Big Al knew exactly what each man's cost was.

The operation ran smooth as silk for six months. Men would shuffle up our alley clutching racing forms, disappearing into the barn where the hot wire carried results straight from the track. Win, place, or show—I learned the language of hope and disappointment, watching losers emerge with torn tickets and dreams scattered like confetti in the ashes.

The bookies knew which horses would win before the races even ran. The fix was always in at the local tracks, and their wire carried all the inside information. It wasn't gambling—it was theater, with predetermined endings and willing marks who thought they had a chance.

But secrets also have a way of unraveling when someone forgets the rules.

The raid came on a Thursday. Someone had forgotten to pay the cops that week—maybe got cocky, maybe just careless. Suddenly our quiet barn exploded like a kicked anthill, with men pouring out every opening in a frenzy of elbows and panic.

I watched from our back door as neighbors I recognized came sprinting through our yard, crushing the anemic forsythia, body-slamming the gate in their desperation to escape. Racing forms scattered like autumn leaves as they ran, these men who'd thought they were just placing harmless bets now fleeing like their lives depended on it.

Fifteen minutes and the place was clean as a whistle. The "Flats Fixed" sign came down, and our barn returned to being just an empty building where termites slowly devoured the wooden beams.

But the strangest secret came as a gift—a massive beach umbrella that appeared in our yard like a peace offering from another world.

"Why do we have a beach umbrella?" I asked my mother, genuinely mystified. We had no beach, no sand, and the umbrella's wooden spike couldn't penetrate our hard-packed soil anyway.

"The bookies gave it to us," she said without looking up from her sewing machine.

"Why would they give us a beach umbrella?"

The silence stretched so long that I thought she might not answer. Then, still focused on her mending: "Because one of the bookies asked if he could date your sister, and I told him no because he's a married man."

That was my mother—woman of few words carrying the weight of dangerous decisions. She'd said no to a mobster, a man who wasn't used to hearing that word from anyone. But she'd done it with the quiet authority of a mother protecting her daughter, and somehow that had been enough.

The umbrella couldn't be returned—that would be an insult. So it leaned against our back window like a striped monument to my mother's courage, proof that sometimes the most powerful men in the neighborhood could be stopped by a simple refusal delivered with unwavering conviction.

The real secret wasn't about bookies or bribes or fixed races. It was about the delicate negotiations that happened in the shadows of working-class life, where respect and fear danced together, and where a mother's "no" could carry more weight than a cop's badge or a bookie's bankroll.

Some protection comes from weapons or trained dogs or paying the right people. But sometimes it comes from knowing exactly when to stand your ground and refuse to be bought, even when the price seems too good to turn down.

The beach umbrella stayed in our yard long after the bookies were gone, a reminder that courage doesn't always roar. Sometimes it just quietly says no and means it, even when saying yes would be so much easier.

Chapter 18:
Suffer the Little
Children

The carousel lamp turned endlessly in the upstairs room, casting blue and white shadows that danced on walls that had seen too much. Below, I sat at the kitchen table, watching my potato pancake mixture turn black while my mother and sisters stared straight ahead, their faces carved from stone.

Something had broken in our house that day. Not the pipes or the windows or the old wooden blinds that never quite closed properly. Something deeper, something that lived in the spaces between rooms, in the sealed doors and locked latches that separated our world from theirs.

The hundred-year-old house had been built by farmers who understood that some doors needed to hold against forces they couldn't name. They'd crafted latches that wouldn't give, hinges that wouldn't bend, wood that remembered its strength long after the trees had been felled.

That night, the house kept its secrets behind stone walls that had been fitted together like prayers. In the basement, evidence lay hidden beneath floorboards—small, soft things that should have been white but weren't anymore.

My mother carried the weight of what she'd seen up those narrow stairs, through the bathroom door that shouldn't have been opened, into a room where a small blue lamp cast shadows that moved like ghosts. She and my sisters had climbed those steps and discovered that monsters weren't just in fairy tales.

The thump, thump, thumping I'd heard through the sealed door hadn't been rats in the walls or the landlady's sister scratching to get out. It had been something else entirely—the sound of innocence being shattered against bathroom fixtures, of trust being broken into pieces too small to put back together.

Decades later, over Orange Blossoms in a restaurant by the Sound, my mother's voice would finally crack open like an egg, spilling the truth she'd carried alone. The words came in fragments—a leg, a bathroom, blood on white tiles—pieces of a puzzle I didn't want to complete but couldn't stop assembling.

The man with the angry skin and Southern accent had tried to burn the evidence in our furnace, but the old farmer's door held fast. My mother's careful habit of keeping that latch locked had trapped him with his secrets, with the weight of what he'd done to something small and trusting.

The house had been a witness and a protector, holding the monster until the men in uniforms could come, swarm into our home like a blue tornado and and take him away. But it couldn't protect us from knowing, couldn't lock away the images that would live behind our eyes like that endlessly turning carousel. I was seven, and I wouldn't know until decades later what had happened.

The restaurant by the water smelled of salt air and fresh beginnings, but I could still taste the metallic memory of that night when everything changed. When I learned that evil wasn't just in the stories the nuns told us about hell and damnation. It was next door, behind thin walls, in spaces where small things should have been safe.

My mother finished her second Orange Blossom and looked out at the sailboats, her hazel eyes holding depths I'd never fully understand. She'd given voice to the secret at last, but we both knew it would never really leave us. Now it came out, in choking bits of revelation. And I wanted to hear, but I didn't want it at the same time. How could anybody be curious about such a thing?

The carousel lamp had stopped turning long ago, but in my mind it spun forever, casting the same blue and white shadows, marking time in a room where time had stopped meaning anything at all.

The house still stands, I suppose, its hundred-year-old bones holding other families' secrets now. But I know what it kept for us, what it witnessed, what it tried to protect with its stubborn doors and faithful latches.

Some secrets aren't meant to be shared. They're meant to be carried, like stones in your pockets, reminders of the weight of knowing too much too soon about what human beings are capable of doing to the smallest among us.

Chapter 19:
Courthouse Days

The witness room was locked from the outside, trapping us in humid silence while the courthouse clock ticked away my childhood. Three weeks of waiting, sweating, and learning that justice had its own cruel rhythm.

"Order a hot meal, dear," May whispered across the greasy table in the coffee shop. "They're paying for it."

But my stomach churned with anxiety. The Salisbury steak swimming in brown goop looked like something already digested. Bright green peas and orange carrots stood out like warning flags against the gray mess on my plate.

May scooped rolls into her napkin while berating her sister Annie, who bent over her food like a frightened animal. "Don't leave anything. We're not paying for it."

Annie's hands shook as she tried to corral the escaping peas onto her fork. She'd been the first suspect—a woman who could barely see a foot in front of her, accused of murder because she was different, defenseless. Even worse, she had a psychiatric history.

"Do you want to go back to the hospital?" May hissed low enough that only our table could hear. "I could've left you there where you belong."

I watched Annie flinch and understood another kind of secret—how cruelty hides behind caretaking, how inheritance money can become chains, how the vulnerable become victims twice over.

Back in the witness room, we sat like prisoners awaiting execution. No talking allowed. No newspapers. No television. Just the rhythmic ticking and the weight of words we weren't permitted to share.

When my turn came, I'd already made my way to the laboratory. The fear made every step an agony. Once inside, the guard pounded on the door as I struggled with my seven-year-old body's rebellion.

"Hurry up, they want you on the stand!"

The courtroom stretched before me like a cathedral of judgment. Hundreds of eyes tracked my shaking legs as I approached the witness chair. The defendant sat at his table, blue eyes drilling into mine with laser precision—a final attempt at intimidation.

"Do you see the person who said something to you here in the courtroom?" the prosecutor asked with his practiced smile.

"Yes." My voice barely escaped my throat.

"Where is he?"

I pointed a trembling finger. "He's over there at that table."

The man scribbled furiously on his yellow legal pad while his three attorneys—three!—wrote their own notes. Why did a monster need so many defenders?

"What did he say to you?"

"Something I can't repeat."

"What do you mean, you can't repeat it?"

"I don't use those kinds of words."

The prosecutor leaned close, smelling of aftershave and hair product. "Whisper it in my ear and I'll tell everyone. That way you won't really be saying it."

Into his cupped hand, I breathed the poison: "He yelled, 'What are you looking at, bitch?' and then looked like he was going to come after me."

The word hung in the courtroom air like a curse I'd been forced to speak. But I hadn't said it—he had. That distinction would matter for years.

"And was that all?"

"No. I saw him hit the baby."

The defendant's neck flushed red, creeping up to his forehead until his attorney whispered something that made him look down at his pad. Even murderers had handlers.

"How did he hit the baby?"

"He raised his hand and hit the baby hard on the side of its head."

"And what was the baby doing?"

"Pushing his cereal off his highchair tray onto the floor."

Seven to fifteen years, the judge decided. Not the electric chair his three lawyers had saved him from, but enough to matter. The woman would wait for him, she told my mother. Wait a year to put a headstone on her murdered child's grave, wait for the man who killed him to get out of prison.

Some secrets aren't about what happened—they're about what people choose to do with what happened. Annie's inheritance stolen by her sister's cruelty. A mother choosing her child's killer over justice. Three attorneys defending the indefensible.

The seven dollars a day we earned as witnesses bought me a crew neck sweater I'd been longing for. Blood money transformed into something innocent, something warm to wrap around a body that had learned too young what adults were capable of.

The real secret of those courthouse days wasn't what I testified to—it was what I learned about the weight of words, how speaking truth can feel like swallowing poison, how justice is a human invention that bends under the pressure of money and politics and fear.

In that locked witness room, we were all prisoners of other people's choices. But some of us would walk free when the trial ended, and some—like Annie, like that woman who would wait—would carry their sentences forever.

The courthouse still stands, its limestone blocks hiding the echoes of all the terrible truths spoken within its walls. But I know what it taught me: that speaking hard truths is both burden and liberation, that seven-year-olds can carry the weight of adult secrets, and that sometimes the real justice happens not in courtrooms but in the courage to use your voice when everything inside you wants to stay silent.

Chapter 20:
A Change of Characters

The pickle jar on the fish store counter held more than dona-tions—it held the neighborhood's complicated relationship with dig-nity. When the runner from Big Al's crew saw it, his face screwed up in disgust.

"What the hell? Jesus Christ, why the hell did you use a pickle jar? The money'll stink and that's not good!"

I crouched in the unused doorway of the liquor store, listening to the argument through the screen door. The manager's voice went high and shaky as he tried to explain it was all they had for collecting burial money.

Mossy was dead. I'd missed it somehow, avoiding that end of the alley like I always did. The cardboard city he'd built was gone, the stairs scrubbed clean, no trace left of the man who'd terrorized and fed the other Bottle Babies in equal measure.

The runner stuffed twenty-dollar bills into the jar with theatrical disgust. "If it's not enough, you let me know because we want to be sure he goes out in style. That's what the boss wants."

Big Al's reach extended even to dead war heroes nobody knew were heroes. The medals they found among Mossy's scattered belongings told a different story than his life in the alley—multiple commendations, campaigns where he'd shown unusual valor. But one medal was missing: the Distinguished Service Medal that should have been there, given the scars across his chest and stomach.

The Bottle Babies—that's what we called the men who lived rough in our alley, sharing cheap wine and whatever shelter they could find. Mossy was their king and tormentor, a man with infected legs who slept in cardboard bicycle boxes and made Mulligan Stew in fruit juice cans. He'd terrorize the others, throw rocks if they got too close to his territory, but he'd also feed them when they were desperate.

The Butcher got his name honestly—not just from his wartime savagery with a bayonet, but from the way he could gut a man's dignity with words. He had one and a half legs, pinning his pants up to show his missing limb when panhandling worked better than hiding it. He'd use crutches and sometimes an eye patch, whatever pulled more coins from passing strangers.

These two men fought constantly over Sneaky Pete and food, circling each other like wounded animals. But they'd also known each other in France during the war, and beneath their daily battles lay something deeper—a connection forged in trenches that neither would ever admit.

The secret was that The Butcher wore Mossy's medal dangling from his torn coat while panhandling. He'd stolen it during a Mulligan Stew dinner, creating a distraction with his crutch while Mossy scrambled to save their spilled meal. The Butcher had already sold his own medal for ten dollars and whiskey money.

The morticians treated Mossy with reverence none of us had shown him in life. They washed his infected legs gently, wrapped them in clean bandages, removed the cardboard from his broken shoes and decided he'd suffered enough—no shoes for eternity, just navy-blue stretch socks on his damaged feet.

"This fellow has been through enough hell," one whispered, glancing at the shabby shoes they'd leave behind.

The new suit, shirt, and tie came from donations Big Al had ordered. The pickle jar's contents covered everything except the respect—that came free, delivered by men who understood what those medals meant, even if they'd never known the man who earned them.

At the military cemetery, they'd lower Thomas Joseph Mosslin into ground that would honor him with a modest white stone. No viewing, no relatives, just the wind-swept burial of a man whose war heroics had been forgotten in the cardboard kingdoms of city alleys.

The Butcher went insane after Mossy died, striking at strangers with his crutch, shouting obscenities on the Avenue. Someone called the cops about "a maniac," and they escorted him to a Veterans' Administration facility where he couldn't sign himself out.

His dirty crutch went into a dumpster, crushed by a garbage truck. The artificial leg he refused to wear gathered dust. But he kept the stolen medal, never admitting it wasn't his, never revealing that his grief over Mossy's death had broken something inside him that couldn't be fixed.

Jimmy disappeared entirely, shy and vulnerable as one of those puppies tossed from car windows. Rube had already died of a heart attack in the fish store, a new baseball in his pocket—a surprise gift for me that never got delivered.

The secret the neighborhoods carry isn't about the crimes or the corruption or the casual cruelties. It's about how death reveals who people really were beneath the roles they played. Mossy the terrorizer was also Thomas the war hero. The Butcher the thief was also a man who grieved his only friend. Big Al the mobster was also someone who understood that respect matters, even for broken men sleeping in cardboard boxes.

The medals pinned to Mossy's chest told the truth his life had hidden. But the missing one, dangling from The Butcher's coat in some veterans' facility, carried a different secret—that sometimes the deepest bonds form between the most unlikely people, and sometimes theft is just another word for love that doesn't know how to express itself.

The pickle jar went back to holding pickles. The alley returned to its normal emptiness. But I learned that day that dignity isn't something you earn or lose—it's something that waits patiently until someone recognizes it was there all along.

Some secrets aren't kept to hide shame. Some secrets are kept because the truth is too complicated for the world that created the need for hiding.

Chapter 21: The Avenue

The dime slipped beneath the paper doily, like a secret being passed between spies. My mother's fingers moved with precision, hiding the tip under the delicate lace pattern while the Woolworth's waitress pretended not to notice.

"Always put the money under the doily," my mother had whispered to me earlier. "Never embarrass a working woman."

I watched the careful dance between customer and waitress—eyes averted, no acknowledgment, the dime disappearing into an apron pocket as dishes were cleared. The whole ritual was designed to preserve dignity on both sides of the counter. I guess I was a little surprised that we were even having lunch here in the five-and-dime store. This was an incredible treat.

That was the secret of The Avenue: everything had a price, but some things cost more than money. This month was exceptional, and my bottle return business was booming, with nickels burning in my pockets.

The day before, I clutched my fifteen cents for a chow mein sandwich—the exact amount I had after a week of collecting deposit bottles. Beer bottles brought a nickel, soda bottles two cents each. It took shopping bags full before I could afford even this small luxury. Today, when my sister gave me a quarter for buying her cigarettes for the past week, I was in for a super treat: a Texas hot wiener.

"What you want, little lady?" The Greek man at the Texas wiener shop looked down at me as I fumbled for my change. Behind him, the grill was blackened with three decades of grease, and coils of flypaper twirled from the ceiling like twisted, old party streamers. A number of "victims" still hung as evidence of its effectiveness. I tried to ignore it.

"I want a Texas wiener, please."

The African-American men at the counter stopped eating, forks suspended in mid-air, staring at the little white girl who had the courage to enter their space. I felt their eyes but pretended not to care. Any disapproving or surprised looks meant nothing compared to that first bite of split hot dog buried under chili, mustard, and raw onions.

"You want it wrapped up, or are you going to eat it here?"

We both knew I wouldn't stay. Five stools, all occupied by men whose presence filled the tiny space. But the question was offered anyway, another small courtesy in the careful choreography of respect.

"Wrap it up, please."

Back at Woolworth's that week, I had navigated the maze of display islands with my chow mein sandwich, careful not to let bean sprouts or cornstarch goo drop onto their merchandise. The saleswoman, sporting a netted hairstyle, watched me.

"Be careful with that sandwich. We don't want it to drop anything on our merchandise or the floor. Understand?"

I understood. I was poor, not stupid. I knew the difference between browsing and buying, between belonging and being tolerated.

The water pistol I wanted cost ninety-nine cents—a fortune that might as well have been ninety-nine dollars. I'd wait for the inevitable markdown, spend three weeks collecting bottles, counting coins on my bedspread like a miser with her treasure.

The secret was that nothing on The Avenue was really about what it seemed. The candy at Loft's wasn't just chocolate—it was a language of sympathy, reserved for hospitals and funerals and births. The chow mein sandwich wasn't Chinese food—it was fifteen cents of belonging, of being able to walk among the shoppers with purpose.

The bootblacks from the shoe shop would nod when they saw me in the Texas wiener place. We recognized each other, children of working families who understood that respect was earned in different currencies depending on where you stood.

My former friends could steal small toys from Woolworth's, fingers quick and consciences clear. But I had the fear of God in me, planted deep by nuns who measured salvation in straight pins and proper posture. I'd pay for what I wanted or do without.

The real secret of The Avenue was simpler than any adult would admit: we were all performing. The waitresses hiding their gratitude for tips, the customers hiding their charity, the shopkeepers pretending not to see the difference between browsers and buyers.

Even I was performing, stretching fifteen cents into an afternoon's entertainment, making a chow mein sandwich last through three aisles of window shopping. Pretending my careful examination of merchandise I couldn't afford was discerning consumer choice rather than desperate longing.

The Avenue taught me that dignity was a luxury some people couldn't afford to lose, so they paid for it in other ways. In hidden dimes and patient questions and the small kindnesses that acknowledged our common humanity without highlighting our different circumstances.

That water pistol I finally bought for seventy cents? It broke in two weeks. But the lesson lasted forever: some secrets aren't meant to be hidden away. Some secrets are meant to be shared through the careful choreography of daily life, in the space between what we can afford and what we need to feel human.

The Avenue's real currency wasn't money. It was the recognition that we all had something to offer, something to protect, something to lose. And in that recognition, poor kids could eat weiners with working men, and working women could accept tips with their dignity intact.

Chapter 22: The Disappearing Neighbor

Every block had someone who drifted in and out like a ghost, and ours had Mr. Callahan. He lived on the third floor of the brick building next to ours, a man with a hat pulled low and a coat worn even in summer. He nodded politely when spoken to, but his eyes rarely lingered. We called him the Disappearing Neighbor, because one day he'd be there, and the next it was as if he'd vanished entirely.

We never saw him carry groceries, never saw him chat on the stoop. Sometimes a week would pass without a single glimpse, and then suddenly he'd reappear, walking briskly down the block as if no time had passed. The adults said he worked nights, that he kept to himself. But we kids wove stranger stories. Frankie swore he was a spy, Dolores claimed he had another family in another city, and Seymour—always eager to add drama—insisted he was hiding from the law. Whatever the truth, his comings and goings were the stuff of our whispered legends.

One evening, as the sun bled gold over the rooftops, I spotted him sitting alone on the stoop, staring at nothing. I gathered my courage and asked if he wanted company. To my surprise, he nodded. We sat in silence, the street alive with kids' laughter and the distant wail of a siren. After a while, he said, almost to himself, 'People think disappearing means you're gone. Sometimes it just means you need space to breathe.' His voice was low, measured, like words carried carefully from somewhere deep inside. I didn't understand it fully then, but the weight of his tone pressed into me.

After that, I watched him more closely. I noticed the lines around his mouth, the way his hands trembled slightly when he lit a cigarette. I noticed that whenever he disappeared, his windows stayed dark, curtains drawn tight. And when he returned, his shoulders looked lighter for a while, as if some unseen burden had been briefly set down. The mystery of him wasn't in where he went, but in why he felt he had to go.

Then one day, he disappeared for good. Weeks passed, then months. His apartment emptied, the door left ajar as movers carried out a battered chair, a mattress, a few boxes that looked too small to contain a whole life. No one said where he went. The landlord shrugged. The neighbors speculated. But no answers came. The Disappearing Neighbor had done what he always did—slipped out of sight, leaving nothing behind but questions.

For a long time after, I'd glance at that stoop, half-expecting to see him sitting there, hat low, eyes shadowed. I never did. Yet the memory of his words stayed. People think disappearing means you're gone. Sometimes it just means you need space to breathe. I came to understand that better as I grew older. Sometimes people retreat not out of malice or mystery, but because the noise of the world grows too heavy, and silence is the only refuge.

Years later, when I find myself needing distance—closing the door, walking alone at night, letting calls go unanswered—I think of him. I wonder if he ever found a place where breathing came easier. I hope he did. Because in his vanishing, he left us more than a puzzle. He left us the secret that disappearing isn't always about absence. Sometimes it's about survival.

Chapter 23: The Secret at Miller's Lake

The summer heat pressed down on everything like a heavy blanket. Jess, Liz, and I had been walking for twenty minutes, sweat sticking our tank tops to our backs, when we finally saw the shimmer of Miller's Lake through the trees.

"Thank God," Jess panted, pushing her dark hair off her forehead. "I'm dying."

Liz laughed. "You said that three times already."

"Because I'm dying three times over."

I was already kicking off my sneakers. "Come on, let's just get our feet wet. Cool off a little."

We'd talked about this on the way over. None of us could swim—not really. A neighbor had tried to teach me when I was seven, but that was years ago. Jess was scared of deep water. Liz had never even tried. But on a day this hot, standing waist-deep in cool lake water sounded like heaven.

The shore was busy with families. Kids splashed in the shallow end while parents watched from beach chairs. A group of teenagers had claimed the dock, taking turns jumping into the deeper water with loud whoops and hollers.

"We'll just go in a little ways," I said, testing the water with my toe. "Just enough to cool down."

The three of us waded in slowly. The water felt amazing against our overheated skin. Pebbles shifted under our feet as we walked deeper, the lake bottom solid and reassuring.

"This is perfect," Liz sighed, the water now up to her knees.

We kept walking, laughing as minnows darted between our legs. The water crept higher—mid-thigh, then to our waists. We were maybe thirty feet from shore, the bottom still firm beneath us.

"Okay, this is far enough," Jess said, but she was smiling, clearly enjoying herself.

I took one more step forward.

The ground gave away.

I dropped like a stone, my surprised yelp cut off as water closed over my head. Panic shot through me as I thrashed wildly, trying to find the bottom with my feet. There was nothing. Just deep, dark water.

I broke the surface, gasping and coughing. "Help! I can't—"

A splash beside me. Liz had stepped forward too and was now flailing frantically, her eyes wide with terror.

"Maya!" Jess screamed from where she still stood in the shallows. But even as she called out, the loose sand under her feet shifted, and she slid forward onto the same underwater cliff.

All three of us were now in over our heads, literally. My lungs burned as I fought to stay afloat. Liz was thrashing so hard she kept going under. In desperation, she grabbed onto my shoulders, pushing me down as she tried to climb up.

"Get off!" I gurgled, but I understood. Liz was drowning.

We both went under. My feet kicked frantically in the dark water, searching for anything solid. My chest felt ready to explode. With a surge of adrenaline, I pushed upward, Liz still clinging to my back.

We broke the surface together.

"Help!" Liz screamed toward shore. "We can't swim!"

But the people on the beach just waved back. Some teenagers laughed and waved harder, thinking we were playing around.

Jess surfaced nearby, coughing up water. "They think we're joking!"

I felt Liz starting to slip off my shoulders. My own strength was fading fast. The shore looked impossibly far away.

"Help us!" all three of us yelled together.

Most people kept ignoring us, but one woman in a blue sundress looked up from her book. She stared for a moment, then suddenly stood up.

She grabbed a bright yellow inner tube from nearby and started walking quickly toward the water. I watched her wade in, pushing the tube ahead of her.

"Hold on!" the woman called. "I'm coming!"

It felt like forever, but finally she reached us. I grabbed the inner tube with shaking hands while the woman helped pull Liz and Jess to the tube's safety.

We all clung to it, breathing hard, as the woman guided us back toward shore. My legs felt like jelly when my feet finally touched solid ground again.

On the beach, we collapsed onto the hot sand, still shaking.

"Thank you," I gasped. "Thank you so much."

"We could have died," Jess whispered.

Liz just nodded, too scared to speak.

The woman in the blue dress smiled at us. "You girls be more careful next time. That drop-off catches people by surprise."

"You saved our lives," I said. "You're an amazing swimmer."

The woman's smile grew a little sad. She looked out at the lake, then back at the three of us.

"I can't swim," she said quietly.

We stared at her in shock.

"I saw you were really in trouble. Sometimes you do what you have to do." She squeezed my shoulder gently. "The secret is knowing when someone really needs help."

As she walked away, the three of us sat in silence, each carrying a new secret of our own—about fear, about courage, and about the stranger who risked everything to save us, even though she was just as scared of the water as we were.

Chapter 24: The Keeper

My mother had a gift for attracting strays—cats, neighborhood kids who needed lunch, and apparently, men who needed a safe place to store their worldly possessions.

The first one showed up on a Tuesday in April. Frank Kowalski stood on our front porch clutching a battered brown suitcase like it contained the crown jewels. His work clothes smelled of hay and horse sweat, and when he smiled, I noticed he was missing a tooth.

"Mrs.," he said, his voice carrying that particular desperation of a man who'd run out of options. "I got a job at the track for the season. Good work, steady pay. But I got nowhere to keep my things safe."

My mother wiped her hands on her apron and looked at the suitcase. It wasn't much bigger than a briefcase, held together with a leather belt because the latches had long since given up. Frank noticed her studying it.

"Just my good clothes and some papers. Nothing that'll cause trouble. I'll pay you five dollars for the whole season if you'll just tuck it somewhere safe."

Five dollars was five dollars. We weren't exactly rolling in money, and Daddy was gone now. My mother's eyes did that quick calculation I'd seen a thousand times—grocery money, utility bills, the growing pile of things we needed but couldn't quite afford.

"Put it in the hall closet," she said. "Behind the winter coats."

Frank's relief was so visible I thought he might cry. He shook my mother's hand with both of his and promised he'd be back for it in October when the racing season ended.

The suitcase sat there for two weeks before the second stray arrived.

Mickey Torrino sold pretzels from a wicker basket on The Avenue. Every evening around six, he'd walk past our house on his way home, the empty basket swinging from his arm. One Thursday, he stopped at our gate.

"Excuse me, ma'am," he called to my mother, who was watering her marigolds. "You wouldn't happen to have a spot where an honest man could store his basket overnight, would you?"

Mickey was small and wiry, with hands stained permanently brown from days in the sun and handling hundreds of pretzels daily. His basket looked like it had been through a war—woven tight but scarred from years of street corners and bad weather.

"I live in a rooming house," he explained. "Tiny room, and the other fellows..." He shrugged. "Well, let's just say a man's possessions aren't always safe there. I'll pay you five dollars a week just for a corner somewhere."

My mother glanced at the basket. It smelled like salt and yeast, not unpleasant at all. She was already calculating again—five dollars a week, plus Frank's five for the season. Together, it would be an unexpected break to ease their stretched budget.

"Barn," she said. "By the workbench."

And so our house became a storage facility for the working men of our neighborhood.

Every morning at five-thirty, Mickey would tap softly on the side door. My mother would hand him his basket, already cleaned from the night before because she couldn't stand to see anything dirty in the barn. Every evening at six, he'd return it, count out his daily earnings at our kitchen table, and slip a portion into the mason jar where my mother kept her "pin" money.

Frank came by once a week just to check that his suitcase was still there. He'd peek into the closet, nod with satisfaction, and sometimes stay for coffee if my mother was in a social mood. He told stories about the horses and the jockeys, about which ones were sure bets and which ones were all flash and no heart.

The routine continued through spring and into summer. Frank's suitcase became part of the furniture, hidden behind my mother's heavy winter coat and a box of Christmas decorations. Mickey's basket took up residence next to my father's old toolbox, cleaned and ready each morning.

I started to notice things about these men that my ten-year-old brain filed away without quite understanding their significance. Frank never mentioned family, never seemed to get mail, never seemed to have anywhere else to go when the track closed for the day. Mickey counted his money with the careful precision of someone who'd learned to make every penny count, but he always had exact change for my mother and never asked for a discount.

One evening in late July, Mickey didn't show up. My mother waited until seven, then eight. She kept glancing at the kitchen window, the way she had when Daddy was late from work.

The next morning, she walked to The Avenue herself, something she'd never done before. She found Mickey's corner empty, another pretzel vendor already setting up in his spot.

"What happened to Mickey?" she asked the new guy.

"Little fella? Heard he got sick. Real sick. They took him to the county hospital yesterday."

My mother stood there for a long time, Mickey's empty basket weighing heavy in her hands. When she got home, she cleaned that basket more thoroughly than she'd ever cleaned anything in her life, then wrapped it in one of her good dish towels and put it in the back of her bedroom closet.

Frank came by that weekend and found my mother sitting at the kitchen table with Mickey's mason jar in front of her.

"He's in the hospital," she said without preamble. "Been saving up for something, but I don't know what."

Frank sat down across from her and peered into the jar. There were maybe forty dollars in small bills and change—Mickey's careful savings from months of pretzel sales.

"Probably medicine money," Frank said quietly. "Or maybe just wanted to die with a little dignity. County hospital ain't exactly first-class accommodations."

They sat in silence for a while. Finally, Frank reached into his pocket and pulled out a twenty-dollar bill.

"Add this to it," he said. "Tell them it's from Mickey's friends."

My mother looked at him with surprise. Twenty dollars was probably half of what Frank made in a week.

"We all got our secrets," Frank said, answering her unspoken question. "Some of us are just better at hiding them than others."

The next morning, my mother took the bus to the county hospital. She found Mickey in a ward with eight other men, looking smaller than ever in the narrow bed. When she pressed the jar into his hands, his eyes filled with tears.

"I was saving for my sister's headstone," he whispered. "She died last winter, and they put her in a pauper's grave. I wanted to give her something nice, something with her name on it."

My mother held his hand until visiting hours ended.

Mickey never came back for his basket. Frank's suitcase stayed in our closet until October, when he appeared one final time to collect it. He looked older somehow, like the summer had aged him more than it should have.

As he hefted the suitcase, Frank paused at our front door.

"Your mother's good people," he told me. "She kept our secrets safe. That's worth more than any five dollars."

After he left, I asked my mother what Frank meant about secrets.

She was washing Mickey's jar, preparing to put it back in the cupboard with her other canning supplies.

"Sometimes," she said, "keeping someone's belongings safe means keeping their dignity safe too. Mickey and Frank, they didn't just need storage. They needed someone to trust them, to treat them like they mattered."

She dried the jar carefully and set it on the shelf. We never knew if the headstone was placed or not, but that didn't matter. What mattered was that Mickey had the wish to honor his sister's memory with a headstone and he worked very hard to try to buy one.

Chapter 25: The Things They Carried Home

The brass button occupied a permanent position in my father's dresser drawer between his cufflinks and his old shining metal shaving mirror. There also were three empty shell casings positioned as small memorials to battles that remained unclear to me.

I used to explain to visitors at home that my father fought in World War I while showing them the artifacts, which made me feel like my father had accomplished something noble and enigmatic. "He was in France." We knew also that he had been there because we had a photograph of him in his military uniform with a snake around his neck. Then there was also the pencil drawing that was so macabre: a skull with men hanging out of the empty eyeholes and the mouth. Why had he drawn that?

My father remained silent when he heard these discussions because he chose not to share additional information about his experiences.

The three brothers, including Uncle John and Uncle Tom maintained their silence about their war experiences.

Family events became filled with conversations about everything except the war experiences of the family members. The family spent their time discussing weather conditions and baseball games and up-coming weddings and job opportunities, yet they avoided discussing either the war or the trenches described in textbooks.

The National Archives provided me with military records, which revealed the actual events of World War I. I was able to uncover not only draft records but also discharge papers and assignments on ships returning from Europe.

I discovered my father's military service record while studying documents at my kitchen table, thumbing through the stack of manila envelopes and photocopied papers.

I held the service record of my father while my hands shook as I read through the official typewritten text.

He had served in the Motor Transport Division at Camp Upton, New York before moving to Motor Pool Supply Base Seven in Le Havre, France.

Motor pool. Not infantry. Not artillery. Not any of the dangerous assignments I'd imagined for years.

The military records showed that Uncle John served in the 42nd Bakery Company at Fort Hamilton, New York before transferring to the Field Bakery Unit at Supply Base Seven in Le Havre, France.

Then Uncle Tom's record in the 42nd Bakery Company.

Bakers. Both of them had been bakers.

The documents stayed in front of me for an extended period while my heart underwent an unexplained transformation. I experienced a peculiar blend of relief and confusion rather than disappointment.

The three brothers fulfilled their military service abroad, yet none of them encountered the combat that I had spent many years picturing.

What about that story my mother had told me that my father returned with shrapnel in his legs that had to be removed at a local military hospital? For years, she would call the hospital and scan the local newspapers for information on his wounds and his service, but nothing ever turned up. The hospital said it had no records of him. Family and the neighbors all said it was because they had lost his records.

Le Havre was not located at the front lines of combat. The supply port operated from behind allied lines to receive shipments of military equipment and food supplies, which supported troops fighting in the interior. My father operated vehicles, which consisted mainly of horse-drawn wagons together with occasional trucks. The soldiers who left for battle received bread from my uncles, who worked in the bakery.

The Sunday dinners with my family became more significant to me after I learned about my father's war experience because people would ask him about his time in combat, but he would shut down his face like a closed book.

He would say, "Some things are better left alone," before we thought that he had witnessed too many terrible things to speak about.

I contacted my cousin Robert, who was Uncle John's youngest son, during the night.

I asked him directly if he knew about their actual military duties during the war. "About what they really did over there?"

Robert remained silent for a brief period before speaking about the bakery work. "I discovered his discharge papers while sorting through his attic belongings several years back. Found his papers."

Why did they choose to keep their wartime experiences hidden from us?

Robert explained to me that soldiers returning from the war expected to share tales of German combat bravery, but they couldn't share their experience of making dinner rolls in France.

I gained insight into the situation at that moment. The brothers felt ashamed because they had survived the war unscathed while other boys from their neighborhood didn't return home.

About the Author

P. A. Farrell is a licensed psychologist, published author of multiple self-help books and videos, former WebMD psychologist expert/consultant, medical consultant for Social Security Disability Determinations, Alzheimer's psychiatric researcher at Mt. Sinai Medical Center (NYC), and an educator who has taught at the college, graduate, and postgraduate levels.

Her influence extends to the pharmaceutical and marketing industries, where she serves as a consultant and has appeared on major TV news programs in the US and abroad. In addition, Dr. Farrell provides continuing education modules for mental healthcare professionals and has contributed to USMLE medical school prep courses. She shares her knowledge through her YouTube channel and her daily contributions to **Bluesky** (@carpenter22,bsky.social) and Medium. com articles. Dr. Farrell's achievements are recognized in *Who's Who in the World, Who's Who in America,* and *Who's Who in American Women.*

A member of the American Psychological Association and the SAG-AFTRA union, Dr. Farrell is a former board member of the NJ Board of Psychological Examiners, a former psychiatry preceptor at UMDNJ, and a former board of directors member of Bergen Pines Hospital (now Bergen Regional Hospital).

Books by Patricia A. Farrell, Ph.D.

How to Be Your Own Therapist

When You Can't Pour From an Empty Glass: CBT Skills for Exhausted Caregivers

The Little Book on Learning Big Critical Thinking Skills

It's Not All in Your Head: Anxiety, Depression, Mood Swings and Multiple Sclerosis

Unfiltered: Beneath the noise of our thoughts lies the true narrative of our minds

Unfiltered Again: A behind-the-scenes look at healthcare, medicine and mental health

When You Can't Pour From an Empty Glass: CBT Skills for Exhausted Caregivers

A Social Security Disability Psychological Claims Handbook: A simple guide to understanding your SSD claim for psychological impairments and unraveling the maze of decision-making

A Social Security Disability Psychological Claims Guidebook for Children's Benefits

The Disability Accessible US Parks in All 50 States: A Comprehensive Guide

Birding in the US NOW!: A birding guide for individuals with disabilities

A Special Request

I f this book has touched your heart, sparked your curiosity, or simply entertained you along the way, I'd be incredibly grateful if you could take a moment to share your thoughts with a review on Amazon or wherever you discovered this book. Your words not only help other readers find books they'll love, but they also mean the world to authors like me who pour their hearts into every page. Thank you for being part of this journey, and for helping stories find their way to the readers who need them most.